# Dedication

*To Clancy Sigal (1926-2017).*
*Let a hundred flowers bloom - no, a thousand.*

# Henry Bladon

# THREEWAYS

*To Kriss,*

*Enjoy !*

*Henry.*

*December 2017*

AUSTIN MACAULEY PUBLISHERS™

LONDON · CAMBRIDGE · NEW YORK · SHARJAH

This is a work of fiction. Names, characters, places and incidents either are the product of the author's imagination or are used fictitiously, and any resemblance to actual persons, living or dead, business establishments, events or locales is entirely coincidental.

A CIP catalogue record for this title is available from the British Library.

ISBN 9781787100787 (Paperback)
ISBN 9781787100794 (E-Book)
www.austinmacauley.com

First Published (2017)
Austin Macauley Publishers Ltd.
25 Canada Square
Canary Wharf
London
E14 5LQ

## Acknowledgements

My thanks to all my readers, to those who read and reread the early drafts, making suggestions and pointing out inaccuracies. I am grateful to Kay Webb for the quirky illustrations that feature in this book, her results perfectly fitted the brief. Thanks to Anne Hamilton for her editorial advice on content and her general hints regarding structure.

I owe a deep gratitude to my wife, Jane, for listening to endless new character developments and other literary minutiae. Her increasingly selective deafness has not diminished her skilful knack of sounding interested. Thanks to my younger daughter, Lucy, who keeps me grounded and is never afraid to tell me when I'm being an idiot. My biggest thanks goes to my elder daughter, Zoe, who must have read *Threeways* a dozen times or more. She never waned in her enthusiasm and always gave me inspirational feedback.

*We could watch the madmen, on clement days,*
*sauntering and skipping among the trim gravel walks*
*and pleasantly planted lawns*

Evelyn Waugh: Brideshead Revisited

$$C_{10}H_{14}N_2$$

(Chemical formula: Nicotine)

$$C_{17}H_{19}ClN_2S$$

(Chemical formula:
Chlorpromazine)

# Chapter One

You can get fixed in this place. Know what I mean? Comfortable and stuck in your ways. When I think about what year it is, they all seem the same, and I have seen so many of them here. Okay, it is 1975, I know that, really. The trouble is, when I think about the passing years, they all seem the same as well. Seasons come and go, but the place rarely changes. I also see the same faces. They get more lines and the hair gets more grey, but that is about the only way of telling the difference.

My ward is not unique, it just happens to be my home. I live here amongst the ash and dirt, the shit and the phlegm. The walls are painted with institutional paint, some of the dour colours are peeling; the high ceilings are stained yellow and brown by the nicotine. Welcome to the innerworld. Welcome to my home. Welcome to Threeways Mental Hospital.

You might want to know how I got here, and perhaps one day I will get to that. I have had some dark days, especially at first. In the early days, I fought the rules, but I learnt that paraldehyde is not pleasant. We all fight at some time or another, though. Even the nurses fight. They fight and argue even when they do not know why they are fighting. Sometimes it is with the patients, who they want to control. Other times it is with the hospital and the rules that, as far as I can see, make them as much a slave to the system as any of us. Sometimes they fight amongst themselves, which could be about promotion. Or they could be bending the rules to avoid punishment by the Nursing Office.

The other day, Ron asked me about a place called Linnet House. He said I could move there from the ward. He said he was a coordinator or an organizer or something like that. It should not have surprised me. A lot of them have started talking about rehabilitation. I remember a time when the staff started taking groups of patients to the town for an afternoon. It was one of their initiatives. They got bored with the idea. Either that or the patients played up and the staff realized they had created a problem for themselves.

I asked Ron what was so bad with Ward 1. Then he said something about Linnet House being more of a home. I must have missed the point. He will forget about it, they always do.

Ron is a nurse, by the way.

Will I ever leave here? That is a question I have not asked for some while, but the conversation made me think. I have spent a lifetime in the company of strangers. I am in my fifties now. Sometimes time passes in a blur, so that I wonder where it has all gone. There are other periods when it drags. In the end, though, life whizzes by. I have known hundreds of patients come and go. Many of them now lie in the old cemetery on the outskirts of the hospital grounds. I have spent time with buzzing in my head, wool in my ears, mashed potato for brains. It all depends on which colour pills they were trying out.

As I say though, one day I will get around to telling more about how I got here.

I have friends and I have other people I know. There are those connected with the hospital and those who visit who cannot wait to get away. As for people in the otherworld, they probably have no idea about what happens here, so let me tell you.

Routine is important in a mental hospital. There are seven hundred patients here, a mix of wandering, dispirited, aimless characters like me. Some with the fireworks inside their heads. That takes a lot of organising. One of the ways they manage our lives is by trying to keep us busy. I suppose they think it keeps us out of trouble.

We come to the Industrial Therapy place three times a week. That's what they call it. We call it the Box Shop. I have been coming here for as long as I can remember, and all we ever do is fold cardboard into boxes. In fact, I am staring at the pile of boxes in front of me. There is not much time to do that, though, because Mr Williams, he is the boss, he has his eye on us. Williams never stops. You would find it hard to believe how a human being could be so mean. I'm guessing that outside the hospital, he would be a nobody, but here he thinks he is a somebody.

His leering face juts out like an unsteady cliff face. I watch him take a backhanded swipe across the back of Sid's head. I feel for Sid. He gets picked on because he's quiet and unlikely to react. I guess that is the case,

13

but who really knows how Williams selects his victims? It could be the fact that Sid has a finger missing and Williams regards him as vulnerable.

Today, it is cold, there is ice on the inside of some of the windows and the faint lighting does nothing to lift the mood. The wooden benches are dirty, and covered in saliva from the drooling patients. The wall clock is inching around. There are times when I think it has stopped.

Williams has confidence in his secluded kingdom. He has only been here for about eight months. Before that, the man who ran IT was not nasty. He died, though, and Williams took over. He used to work on the maintenance but he fell off a ladder and now he has a limp. That does not stop him wearing high heels, though. They are all the rage at the moment. A lot of the male nurses wear stacked heels. Williams does it because he is small and wants to appear big.

Williams finds it easy to be a bully because he knows that nobody else is ever likely to visit. The Box Shop is too out of the way, and other staff are disinterested. As long as we come and go, and the products are churned out, nobody cares. Apart from the delivery drivers, nobody comes here. A mental hospital is no place to hang around.

From time to time as it does now, a hacking cough breaks the silence. But even that is not allowed, and Williams shouts at the patient, telling her to shut up. He does circuits of the benches, daring anyone to look up. I don't often look up, but I have watched the tormenting of my friend throughout the morning. It is just another way that they control us. We are nobody.

There is a patient concentrating, occasionally wiping his nose with his sleeve. Sometimes he is too late and a dribble of snot falls onto the bench. Williams doesn't see this happen, which is just as well. Instead, he rounds on Sid again.

'You're useless,' he says. 'That bloody great beard gets in your way. It's like a rug. Why don't you chop it off?'

Sid is proud of his beard. I watch him cower.

'You're here to do my work, get on with it,' says Williams.

Since when this was his work, I don't know. I thought this was hospital therapy. Williams thinks he owns the IT Department. It is his area of influence. This place is all about controlling others and he is a good example of how power can go to the head.

Eventually the morning is over, and along with the other patients, me and Sid make our way back to our ward for lunch. The sky is overcast and the wind is biting.

'Are you okay, Sid?'

'Yeah.'

'Does your head hurt?'

'Nah. I've known worse.'

I know he is saying that because it upsets me to see. He is a friend, and no one likes to see a friend get hurt.

'I wonder what's for lunch?' he asks me.

Monday is sausages, he ought to know that, he has been here long enough to know that. It is always sausages on a Monday.

I spark a cigarette and offer him a light for his. The hospital cigarettes are harsh and the smoke can burn the back of the throat. There are times when you can get a different brand, the type that you might see on the TV or in a magazine, but you need money for that. Or you have to barter hard. Like I say, most of the time we are stuck with the ones they hand out here. Once you get past the initial intake, they do their job and the calming wave more than compensates. Today, the cool air makes it worse and I cough when I inhale the smoke.

We walk past the clock tower. The clock says ten to one, but I know it is always five minutes fast. It has been for as long as I can remember. It stopped once, whether that was maintenance or mechanical failure, I am not sure. When it restarted, it was still five minutes fast.

'Are you going to music?'

He drags on his cigarette and stops, as if he is thinking hard. I know he is going to say yes. How do I know? Because he always goes to Ron's music group on a Monday. We both do. Mondays are sausages and then music.

Sid laughs, because he knows what I am thinking.

'Come on,' I say. 'Let's get our grub before it's all gone.'

I look at the familiar red stonework of the hospital as we enter the main corridor side by side. The wind wants to find a warm space and tries to follow us in. Some days the corridors are warmer than others. Sid starts to rub his hands together, partly because of the cold, partly in expectation of his lunch. The sounds of our heels echo up from the floor and into the curved ceiling. The light shades are made of tin and the bulbs only give off a weak glow. Patients stand about here, and some of the old boys just wander from one end to the other all day long. Every day. They look like they are dragging about an empty soul, staring into a sheet of grey. Or listening to the thunder of their white noise, their brains bashing on the inside of their skull. One of them has been marching back and forwards for as long as I can remember. There are times when I wonder whether he is searching for a secret passage, a portal through which he can escape to another world, if only for a few hours. What a nice thought.

It takes four hundred and forty-five steps to get back. When we reach the ward, we go through the door and the smell of sausages wafts towards us. The lunch delivery from the main kitchens has already arrived, but we are not too late. I go to the male dormitory to dump my overcoat. There is another dorm for the ladies at the other end of the ward. The dorms don't have a lot of furniture, what with all the beds. Thanks to the environmental efforts of recent years and the attempts to create calm in the place, the beds are well-spaced now. And there are pictures on the walls. The arrangement is set into a private space. But privacy is really an illusion. Each space has its own metal bed, bedside locker and small wardrobe. There is more peeling wall paint in our dorm, and it is a drab grey. In the female dorm, it is a pallid lavender colour. The temperature is either icy cold or tropical heat. Maintenance staff are often taking temperature measurements and fiddling with the old pipework.

I leave my coat on the bed and make my way back to the day room, where a patient is complaining. I say complaining, he is muttering to himself.

'Fucking bastards,' he is saying. I have no idea why. He could be talking to a person I cannot see.

Until the meal is announced, I sit myself down in a vinyl chair and relax with another fag. On the table, there are ashtrays, all of them full. As soon as the domestic staff empty them we restock them. I wonder for a moment why we don't make ashtrays in the Box Shop. That would be much more useful here, because there are always ashtrays, loads of ashtrays. All of them full of fags smoked right down to the filter. They have to be smoked all the way because if they are not, they are reclaimed for what tobacco is left. Smoking is the past-time of choice here. Every room on my ward is affected by nicotine. The colour of the walls in each room has been transformed into smoke-stained streakiness. Even the consultant's office. So why don't we make ashtrays at the Box Shop? I suppose it would not be called the Box Shop then, would it?

'Lunch.'

A nurse hollers the word through the serving hatch, it is the signal for a scramble. It helps to have sharp elbows in this place, or you could go hungry.

The nurse slops the mash into my plate, and three sausages are added and then some gravy. A few peas get ladled on as well and I leave the line to claim my usual spot.

It is all over in a trice. Some of the patients move their head close to the plate and scoop the food in. A lot of them don't have teeth, thanks to poor hygiene and medical experimentation.

'I wish we could do something about Williams,' I say to Sid, who is sitting next to me.

He ignores me, intent on finishing his lunch and getting some of the chocolate sponge pudding.

I have often thought that we should do something, but I know the chance of success is limited. Perhaps that is the real reason why Sid doesn't answer. I take a drink from my plastic beaker. They used to give us glasses in the old days, back in the sixties, but too many of them got smashed by angry patients.

Before I know it, I am lining up again. Time for two white pills and a yellow one.

### Pills

*Give me the pills, to cure all my ills,*
*The yellow the pink and the white.*
*But they mess up your brain, and make you insane,*
*And take away all of your fight.*

# Chapter Two

What was he expecting? This is a group of people used to routine and repetition. We are not likely to propose a revolutionary change to his programme. Staff nurse Ron has a high KQ. That's how I occasionally refer to people around here. KQ stands for 'Kindness Quotient'. I adapted the idea from a student nurse who was made to do an IQ test with the patients on the ward. The staff may have been bored that week. Or it might have been a way of reminding us that we are not as good as them. I suppose it could even have been a new initiative to diagnose the patients. Who knows? Anyway, the KQ scale is my way of grading the feelings of those I come into contact with. Ron has a high KQ, and like I say, he's a nice enough nurse. I love music and I like his weekly group. But really, what was he expecting when he asked us about the programme? Most of us didn't even know there *was* a programme. We get enough of that with the Box Shop and other stupid places like Occupational Therapy. Some patients only come in here to sleep.

Ron makes a noise about planning more sessions, making suggestions for future themes. He is talking about Spanish guitar and Big Band classics. He mentions Rod Stewart. I nod at him. Ron, not Rod Stewart, but I am thinking about something else. He decides to continue with the music, which today is Simon and Garfunkel. It seems that now that we've got the short discussion out of the way, the group is ready for a bit of peace and quiet. For my part, I am happy with the tones of *America*, *Bridge Over Troubled Water* and *The Sound of Silence*. There's nothing in the melody that will hurt my brain. And there are days when my brain hurts.

In the Blue Room, the record player sits on the side, behind Ron. Do you know that the Blue Room isn't actually blue? No. It was, but now it is a pale-pink colour. The paint is not peeling in this room yet because they only painted it last year. We are all facing him in a semicircle. It is our version of the ward round, when they—the staff, that is—all get together to talk about us. The Blue room is warm. Put that with the medication and the lunchtime food, and sleep is inevitable. I once watched Ron fall asleep too. That was funny.

Marjorie, the lady who comes over from Ward 9 simply to scrounge fags, she has come and gone. She swears at Ron all the time, calling him a bastard, but he still gives her cigarettes. Doesn't he know anything about reinforcement? I thought they taught the nurses that stuff when they were students. It is the same every week. She buggers off as soon as she gets what she wants.

Neil is sitting to my left. He laughs every so often. He is an idiot. I do not mean in the way of trying to make him sound like an imbecile—which is actually an old-fashioned word they still use to classify some of the patients here—I mean it in a way that he does not always know what you are talking about. This doesn't bother him, or most other people, for that matter. Best of all, Neil is inoffensive. His hair is always a mess and his shoes have food and coffee and ash ground into them. This is occasionally made worse by his toilet habits, which can spill other unpleasant things onto them. There are times when his shoes are soaked in urine. I think the shoes were brown when they started their life, but that would be a guess.

'Do you know Graham, Ron? This bloke I met, he gave me a light from his lighter, he said would I like see...the vicar?' Ron is trying to stay with the story, such as it is. The structure is fragmented and the pace and pitch of Neil's voice keeps altering. He restarts. 'The vicar, he cut...an inch off his grass. He had to mow his lawn.'

I feel there is something ethereal about Neil, as if a distant spirit. He is a detached entity, projected through time from another dimension. I wonder whether he has been sent through time, sailing light years to mess with Ron's sensibilities. He could be toying with him, testing him, operating on another wavelength.

Ron listens. Neil grins his satisfaction and goes quiet.

'Oh my God!' Marjorie has made her way back, and has heard enough. 'Can't you shut him up?'

Ron puts his forefinger on his lip like a librarian.

'Bastards,' says Marjorie. She starts rummaging in her handbag. Then she laughs for no reason.

Sid is here too, stroking his beard. He always comes to music with me, and we sit next to each other. Music is a respite from the monotony of somewhere like the Box Shop and the cruelty of Williams. I cannot remember how long Ron has been doing the group, but it must be two years, on and off. He is proud of his work. He doesn't ever boss people about, not like some of the other nurses. He is kind, which can work against him, but he believes in trying to help. That's what nurses are really supposed to do, isn't it? Shame some of his colleagues do not see it like that.

Sometimes Sid is really fed up. In a music group a while back, when Ron had asked the group about whether he could make improvements to the format, Sid's response was blunt. 'It's pointless. We're all going to be dead soon. This place is a living hell.' I wondered at the time whether Sid might have had a point.

The funny thing is, none of the other group members are affected by Sid's expressions of morbid negativity. Even a lady who, until recently had been convinced that the porters were planning to kill her. That day, she made a solitary comment. 'The messages are strong today.' She was staring straight ahead. Then she looked at Ron. 'Messages?' He asked. That was an open goal. 'Yes, the messages,' she said, not quite getting why Ron was being so stupid. 'The messages from the music.' Ron just smiled and nodded.

Mike is here also. He hangs about with me and Sid as well; he is learning the guitar. Well, I say learning, it is more like musical murder. But at least he is trying.

In the groups, there is more music that some of us want to hear. Other patients use it as a temporary anaesthetic.

Marjorie dribbles. She laughs when she sees the spit fall onto her jumper. Neil fidgets. Sid stares at his hands, which are in his lap. Ron looks about as if waiting for a miracle. I know he means well, and in that respect, he stands out from a lot of the other nurses. His energy is to be applauded, particularly considering that he's been at Threeways some time. I do not know exactly how much time, you can only guess. It is not as long as I've been here, that would be almost impossible, but he has been here a long time. Of course his enthusiasm could be due to boredom. I would not want to suggest that the other nurses are all evil or something. Or that in any other sphere of life they would have a need to dictate living standards. But they have their routines and rules. They face a daily sense of imposed order and end up feeling the need to capitulate to a higher power. Their desire and enthusiasm is overwhelmed by the importance of operation. I know a lot of the nurses find the work here monotonous. Try living here, I always want to say. But I don't.

Rain is hitting the panes like water darts trying to break into the room. I look out at the grey sky. It is a metaphor for our existence. It isn't a thing I consider very often, if ever, but after Ron started talking about his plan to get people out of Threeways, it got me thinking. It is ridiculous, of course, but now I know about it, I can't imagine how it would be for me. I have been stuck here too long. I have no idea about how to get accommodation. He said the patients might have to learn to cook, and that is a scary thought. Why did he choose me?

The music plays. Edward is smiling and staring at the ceiling, Sid has fallen asleep. I light a cigarette and watch the end glow between my fingers as I drag another refreshing intake.

### *Spirit of Love*

*I finally knew*
*The spirit of love*
*Which betrayed by a tear*
*Would banish all fear*

# Chapter Three

Here I am again. The Industrial Therapy Unit, that's a grand name for a crappy building. It is tucked away at the far end of the grounds beyond the chapel and past the gardens. Every time I see the grey stone building with its blue slate-tiled roof, my heart sinks. Some of the tiles are missing. Inside, it smells of damp and body odour. I wish we were in the boiler room sometimes. The boiler room is warm, as you might imagine, but it is also light. The roof is in the shape of a tall steeple with skylights on one side. It is a while since I went there. They have massive machinery and thick iron pulley chains there. It's really quite exciting. Not like IT. Not like the Box Shop.

We get tokens for our efforts here, surrogate cash. We can exchange them at the patients' social club for tea and coffee, or, most likely, cigarettes. Token effort, that's what we make. Haha, that has never occurred me before. Do they think such a modest payment motivates us to keep going through the morning? In a way, it does, but really, we are simply in passive agreement due to the compulsory nature of our attendance. It's beneficial, they say, those who make such decisions.

Some mornings, the time limps along. I learned long ago to shut off my mind and just stick to the tedious duties of my task. If there is a skill that you learn as a patient at Threeways, it is to defocus. Today

I have found another way to deal with the monotony. I am imagining a Monopoly board, the last time we played on the ward. I can recall my position and my properties, and I can even manage to remember roughly how much money I had. Mike was being the banker and I am pretty sure he was awarding himself some extra rents, but I let that go. This way of drifting my mind, the boxes and the tedium are pushed out to the edge of my thoughts. Other times, I recite a Philip Larkin poem in my head. He is my favourite poet. These are the ways I manage to transport myself out of the IT department and into another place. It makes for a more pain-free experience.

That is not the case for Sid, who is wincing even before the hand slaps his head. The noise as the hand catches some bare flesh on his scalp is like a fish hitting a foredeck. The sound goes through me. I can only imagine how it feels for Sid.

Some days, I just wish he would react and hit back at Williams. I wish our previous boss had not died. Just as I am thinking this, a woman at the far end of the room starts shouting.

Williams tell her to be quiet but I can see that will not work.

'Leave me alone,' she says, as he gets near. Then she takes off one of her shoes and throws it at him. It hits him in the stomach and he recoils.

'Now just you stop it, Angela.'

'Fuck off,' she screams. 'Leave me alone.'

Angela gets off her stool and marches towards Williams. The click of her heel alternates with her stockinged foot. Williams has already gone into his office, leaving the path clear for her to pick up her shoe, get her coat, and slam the door to the department.

I realise that my heart has been pumping faster as I watched. I am glad she didn't get a slap off Williams I know what he did, he went into his office to phone the ward.

We all know the punishment for aggression, and it doesn't matter what caused it. In the old days, before the new medicines, they would chuck patients into padded cells. Or they would use a straightjacket. The jackets became less common over the years after I arrived, but the cells are still here. Only now, they talk about cooling off. It still amounts to controlling the behaviour they don't care for, though. You see? This place is all about controlling others.

Depending on what mood she is in when she arrives back, Angela might get transferred to a secure ward for a while. The secure wards have high windows, which makes me think of that poem by PL.

This was an unusual event. We normally don't bother to argue here. We leave that for other times when the reaction we get from the nurses is more fun. Williams is too unpredictable for that.

After the department goes silent again, Williams reappears. He has a smirk on his face, which is never a good sign.

Why do we call it the Box Shop? That's a good question. It is obvious when you think about it. I told you we fold bits of cardboard into little boxes, so there you have it. Actually, we have only been doing the boxes for about five years. Before that, we put labels on matchboxes. Now that's ironic, don't you think?

When I first came to Threeways, this place didn't exist. They converted an old machinery store about ten years ago and there are times when I can still smell the oil. Before the Box Shop, they didn't bother much with work. We had the farm, where we dug in potatoes and grew beans, but the focus was on keeping us busy, rather than work. We had recreational activity, but these things go in phases, and they are dependent on the motivation of the staff and the desire to engage. When your head is full of negative thoughts or worry, you don't really feel like playing badminton on the lawns. Trust me.

We carry out the tasks without thinking. The scurrying, rustle of cardboard is our equivalent of soldiers marching on a parade ground.

We don't care where the products are going, or how much money the unit will make. We don't care that the idea of sending us here is an excuse to get us off the wards, despite what they claim. It's just part of Threeways life. You accept the drudgery of a place like IT. You have to. You can't fight it. Where would that get you? They dislike trouble makers in Threeways. Take your pills, go to work, get up when they say. It's all part of the control.

Williams is now prodding Sid. It is retribution for what happened with Angela. Williams didn't get his chance to retaliate.

'Get on with it,' he says.

Sid puts his head down a little further.

'You're fucking useless, d'you know that?'

Maybe Sid does, but maybe he just wants to get out of the Box Shop and back to the ward.

'Fucking useless,' repeats Williams. He cuffs Sid on his ear.

My hand tightens on the box in front of me. In a moment the box crushes in. I don't know my own strength, sometimes.

Williams never seems to use his anger for anything more than a self-serving intimidation. I mean, some people, when they get angry, they can run faster or accomplish a task by making the energy into a positive force. It gets redirected and channelled. Williams is more about the destructive nature of rage. It is eating him from the inside as well, because I can see it start to appear at the surface of his physical existence. I am starting to see through the increasing transparency of his shell. More warts, more brown spots on his face and hands. More yellow in his eyes.

It is a relief when Williams clomps off to his office to put another shot of brandy in his coffee. He will sit in there for a while, his feet on the desk, smoking another cigarette and flicking the ash on the floor. I know we are safe until the rattle of the door knob and the sound of the creaky hinges tells us that he is ready for another round of intimidation and insults.

In case you didn't already guess, Williams has a low KQ, by the way.

One of these days I am going to say something. I would love to say something. The problem is, as I think I've already told you, that just marks you out as trouble. I have been here long enough to know that.

The clock drags round to twelve-thirty. Me, Sid and Mike leave the department and walk back together. The January chill is particularly bad today, so we all have our heavy coats on over our jackets. My toes are numb inside my old hospital shoes. I call them hospital shoes, but only because they got them for me. There was a time when there was a cobbler in the hospital who mended heels and patched the leather soles worn from pacing the concrete paths around the grounds.

Mending soles. Shame that is the wrong spelling.

There is a woody smell from Mike's cigar. He seems to be taken with the idea of smoking cigars, but when it comes down to it, he will smoke anything. I once knew a patient who was caught by a nurse smoking a pound note. The nurse asked her why she didn't go and buy some fags instead. It was a good point. Twenty fags was about sixpence at the time. I wonder if the desperation got to her.

Another patient walks past us and spits a green glob which splatters onto the concrete. I heard the coughing before he reached us and for once it isn't me. He walks on, surrounded by a cloud of his cigarette smoke.

'Are you okay, Sid?' I ask.

'Yeah.'

His tone suggests he isn't. He is resigned. I know when Sid is feeling bad way before he starts with his depressed commentary. I can hear it in his voice. Soon, he will be saying, 'Roll on death,' and proclaiming himself one day closer to the grave.

'Ears are ringing a bit,' he adds.

'Could be worse,' I say, making a joke and pointing at Mike.

Mike is carrying his guitar over his shoulder, in a special carrying bag. He has threatened to play when we get back to the ward. I can't think of a good enough excuse not to listen yet, but I have until we reach the day room and I am working on it.

'You know,' I say to Mike, 'I sometimes feel like I could smash that guitar over Williams' head.'

The other two stop dead. Mike laughs, until he realises that it's his guitar I am talking about. Sid stares at the path and nods.

# Chapter Four

Poor Sid. He's on conversational terms with few, and friends with even fewer. He has the spirit of Goya, dark and sad. Or Rothko. At art therapy, he once depicted himself as a graveyard. The depth of his sadness can be represented by a Mahler symphony. I am pretty sure that Edward would be proud of me for that description. Possibly Ron, too. Although I am not sure Ron would remember playing Mahler at music. I might be wrong but I think that was the session he fell asleep. I think of Ron as like a Turner painting: vague and dreamy. Dreamy enough to come up with a scheme to move me out of Threeways,

Some people have a tough time, and life has not been kind to Sid. He was a machine worker. He has had depression for most of his adult life and that eventually brought him to Threeways, where most days are a blur of empty nothingness. We could call him Sad Sid, but we don't. When he is really bad, he takes to his bed and stays under the covers regardless of the best efforts of the staff. Those that dare approach are given a clear message.

Sid's approach to people reminds me of a thing I read in a book. It said: *L'enfer, c'est les autres,* which apparently means you can't bear other people. For example, last week, a student nurse came to Ron, saying that Sid was under the sheets and wouldn't get up. He had warned her off. 'I wish I had a machine gun...You're no better than the Nazis...Six million people died in the Holocaust, you're no better than that.' This is normal for Sid when he is feeling bad, and as a deterrent, it is pretty powerful. Her perseverance didn't improve the situation. 'You're all machines of the state,' said Sid, following up with his ultimate cry of despair; 'Roll on death.' Ron calmed the student, of course. He did his best to explain the condition and counselled her on her approach.

'He detests the hospital,' he told the student, who looked close to tears. 'Don't take it personally.'

The poor girl, she was bewildered. It was hard not to notice her shaking hand and her bitten nails. She is only a young thing. It is unfair how they thrust these kids into such a cauldron of human misery and misbehaviour. Her wrists are thin and delicate, too delicate for here, I fancy. Her face is plain, no make-up, probably under pain of death from the matron if she sneaked in any mascara. She will toughen up. They usually do, some of them by too much.

Sid is confusing. His expressions of hatred for the system prove his energy, in spite of his apathy. The counter argument is that the same hospital system he loathes has Sid looked after and cosseted, like a young bird protected by a caring mother. But he is another statistic, caught up in a personal sadness.

Sid once told me about his past, how he worked in a factory in Cowley, fitting car parts. That's where he lost his finger, by the way. He was a reliable worker, he told me that. The sixties were not without difficulty.

He said he felt isolated at school and this carried through into early adulthood. He found it difficult to form lasting relationships, and he was awkward in the company of others. He said everyone around him seemed to be so confident. Sid tried drugs, not like the ones they give out here, I mean hippy type drugs. He told me he smoked dope. He told me that helped with his shyness. He also took LSD, which apparently wasn't so good.

Sid hates authority. It is probably something to do with his childhood, I expect. He calls the police a bunch of bully boys, but he has never told me why. Perhaps he has a point. He has never told me the reason for his loathing of life. One of the theories, suggested by a long-forgotten psychotherapist, was that Sid has an antipathy towards authority as a result of incomplete bonding with his father. As I say, though, long-forgotten.

There is irony about the violent imagery, because Sid is a pacifist. He would not cause harm to anything. I think they class him as agoraphobic, but like all these things, it is never that simple. It's a funny life, really, when you think about it. The tainted blood that runs about our imperfect beings is a challenge to those who peer in. They fail to appreciate the complexity of existence. We could shout, sometimes we do, at each other, at ourselves, at the sounds in our heads. It is nothing but a walk on a wet night in a lovely forest.

As you might expect, psychiatry has given him its best shot. But surprise surprise, anti-depressant medication and ECT have made little difference. So here he is, by my side in a mental hospital.

There is a noise from the other side of the room.

'I'm having you all *arrested*!' The anger in the last word is concentrated on the second syllable. I see Ron peer through the serving hatch, Martin has turned his chair to face the wall. His arms are resting on his knees, which in turn allow him to support his jaw on his hands. I get up to go towards the serving hatch.

'And you can bugger off!'

Of course I ignore him, he does not mean what he says. Ron calls over to him.

'Okay, Martin?'

'Nah, I'm bloody not! I'm seeing someone about this…the IRA will blow you all up, and the SAS, they're sending a sniper. This place will be a pile of BRICKS!' He continues to stare at the wall. 'And the Royal family are all going to be blown up as well, and Buckingham Palace and Windsor Castle, and all the nurses…And this place will be rubble because I can do,' at this point he pauses for breath. 'WHAT. I. WANT!'

Ron passes me two cups. I go over to Martin. 'Want a cuppa?'

'Haha. They're all going to prison.'

I am amused that Martin does not seem to include me in the potential arrests.

'Three sugars?'

I nod and smile. Martin cackles.

I take my coffee and wander into the day room for a smoke. When I place my mug on the table, I notice

39

the crack in the top and the dribble of coffee running down the side.

### *(For Sid)*

*Black – it's all he can see*
*Heavy and slow.*
*Chained, he seeks the code*
*That could save him.*

*Deceived by the dragging of time*
*Passing as eternity*
*A black hole from which he cannot escape*

*He wears his mask of pain.*
*And sadness,*
*Weighed by the anchor he must support*
*Every day of his life,*

*His confused head*
*Is full of nothing.*
*The sun still shines, the wind blows too*
*He does not notice.*

# Chapter Five

I am dragged back from the density of the dark blue depths of sleep. My muscles are stiff when I awake. My back is sore and my neck feels like a twisted rope. My eyeballs are heavy and reluctant to open. I do not have an alarm clock. The symphony of the hospital is normally enough to rouse most patients. First we hear the birds outside, then we hear the arrival of the staff. We hear the cars outside and then the jangling keys and banging doors. That is when the other men start to stir and as they do they cough in a variety of tones. The firecracker cackle from across the dorm is met in call-and-response style by the lurching bellow of a sea lion. I join in and hear a syncopated rumble that begins deep within my chest wall, surging to a crescendo. The contents resurrected from the blackened innards of my lungs.

Buzz, crackle, hum. The lights are on: time to get up. My muscles are aching and my mouth is dry save for the phlegm which barely moistens my tongue. I swing my feet out of the bed and they hit the floor that has been chilled by the winter air. I put on my socks and shuffle to the toilet. As I begin to shave, I think about the summer, when overmedicated patients wander the grounds. They lay down like wilted weeds. The summer fête comes and goes and we have a barbecue and things feel happy. The winter can be harsh.

The breakfast rush is over quickly. I listen to a patient called Ralf ranting, having a mad conversation with himself. Before, he was telling the ward that he is Henry VIII, and that the doctor he saw in the car outside the administration block is Jack the Ripper. It makes you realise that there really is no end to life's variations.

'I started the universe,' he says. 'Not her, with the pale bucket in her hand. The sailor is married to the owner by the edge of the wall.'

For a moment, it reminds me of the surrealist poetry I read once. The man continues his chatter.

'She thinks they're going to leave and then come back. It's all I can do; I'm as poor as a cat, but I take what the doctor prescribes for me.'

Threeways monologue. We hear so much of it here. There are days when you cannot get away from the pronouncements. Today is going to be one of them, because Martin is talking to one of the nurses, trying to convince her that his insides will soon be on the outside.

'My kidneys have turned to jelly,' he says.

The nurse nods and smiles.

'My colon is radioactive and it's poisoning my heart.'

I cannot help but be impressed that Martin knows what a colon is. It occurs to me that if Martin had complained like this in the old days, they might have removed his colon in the belief that it was the cause of his madness. He starts clutching theatrically at his chest. The nurse, like the rest of us, has seen this performance a thousand times.

'Martin, why don't you go and have a cigarette?'

'My thigh bones are broken. And my ankles. My ribs are like splinters pushing through my skin. I'm going to be in a great deal of pain today.'

'Martin.' The nurse's tone is inquiring, lifting at the end so to cause a change of direction in the exchange. You can't help but admire the artful subtlety of some of them.

Martin pauses and places his hand over his chest. 'I'm having a heart attack now.' The nurse looks at him from under her eyebrow. 'I don't have any cigs, nurse.'

She reaches into her pocket and hands him a cigarette from her packet. Martin turns and lets out a huge fart. It sounds like a small scooter accelerating away.

'That's my reward, is it?'

'Sorry, nurse.'

Martin disappears, chortling to himself. I am never sure whether he is genuinely worried about his welfare or simply playing a game. I don't think the doctors know either.

Talking of doctors, I see Dr Metcalfe arrive on the ward in his white coat. His shoes are certainly shinier than Neil's, probably because he doesn't piss on them. As always, Dr Metcalfe is wearing a three-piece-suit. And he has a gold watch on a chain. His dad was a psychiatrist here too. I knew Dr Metcalfe pretty well. Young Dr Metcalfe is now about sixty years old, he will

44

probably retire soon. He comes to direct the ward round on a Wednesday and all the other staff panic, including the junior doctor. It is really quite funny. They always wear their white coats, the head doctors. By that, I mean the senior ones, the ones in charge. Although you might call them doctors of the head as well. Their coats signal superiority. They clack along the corridors with the junior doctors trailing behind. That's what this place is all about, the power of the white coats and the corridors.

The head nurse on my ward is a male nurse. He has a fat head and rolls of skin on his neck. His KQ varies. There are times when he makes a special fuss and he seems scared of getting things wrong. This always makes me laugh because he has been head nurse of the ward for many years. He has curly blond hair and a big belly and always has his shirt sleeves rolled up. In fact, a lot of the male nurses seem to do that. I also remember *his* dad. He was just as large, and he was a big bully to go with it. Normally, the head nurse sits in the office smoking and reading the papers. Sometimes, if he wants to chat about how shitty his day has been, he uses the office telephone to call other charge nurses and that normally makes him start laughing. Charge nurses are often men in Threeways, and most of them are friends with the head nurse on my ward. There are plenty of other wards in Threeways. All of them are full of people with a mixture of stories about how they ended up here. In the past, patients came here and stayed until they died, only moving to a geriatric ward when they couldn't remember how to feed themselves. Now, I see patients who come and go and come back again. Some of them come for ECT in the day. I don't know why they don't just stay. Maybe because they have a family or a place to go back to. That wasn't the case in the old days.

The head nurse puts his feet on the desk and occasionally orders the student nurses to fetch him a coffee. Not on Wednesdays, though, because on Wednesdays he has to do some work and get everything ready for Dr Metcalfe.

The funny thing is, if it were not for the occasional new patient or someone who has decided to be threatening during the week, the meeting could be over in no time. I know they call people long-stay patients like me 'incurable'. They used to call us 'chronics'. Or is that the other way round? Anyway, what do they know? I mean, what is even wrong with me? When I think back, I have seen dozens of different doctors and have been diagnosed with so many illnesses. Would you care to see my case notes? I bet not, because the files are huge. It makes me wonder whether Ron is familiar with all the details. He will probably have to be if he wants to convince them to let me out. But even if he is, they do not tell the whole truth. They only tell the truth as they see it, which is one side of a story.

I think I already told you that in our music, the chairs in the Blue Room get arranged into a semicircle. They do the same for their ward round, but it has a different meaning. The head nurse always puts his next to the psychiatrist. They go into the room for between one to two hours. I don't know exactly what they talk about, but it can't be very interesting as a lot of them come out rubbing their eyes looking like they need a bed to sleep in. Also, if they were any good, they would be curing the patients, and then they would not need the hospital. Actually, maybe I have hit onto something there, because they don't want to put themselves out of a job, do they? I wonder if Ron has thought of that.

I have a good idea what they say about me in the meetings. I guess that the usual conversations don't last all that long. 'How's Tim?'

'Oh, the same as usual, doctor.'

'Do we need to change anything?' (He will say that to justify the conversation.)

'No, I don't think so, doctor.' That would be about it. What else could they say? If it weren't for the ward meetings, we would get entirely forgotten, blending as we do into the tapestry of the hospital. They are duty bound to mention us in their meetings. Ethics, or something like that. They don't really care for our existence, and I don't blame them. We barely notice ourselves sometimes.

Maybe this is about to change Ron is the supervisor, or organizer, I cannot remember the term. His project might change the format of this discussion. Of course, he will have to convince people like Dr Metcalfe, and that is never easy.

After their meeting, when they have wandered out in different levels of tiredness, the nurses go straight to

47

their office. That is their special hiding place, where they laugh and joke together. It is the place where patients who interrupt their peace are regarded as a nuisance. They are not all bad, and I am probably making them sound lazy. It really depends when you interrupt them. Handover times are strictly out of bounds. The head nurse always wears a bunch of keys on his waistband. Like I said, he likes to read the paper, or chat to his friends in the other wards on the hospital phone. It is a funny thing, because, just like the fact that I know most faces in the hospital, many of the staff also know each other. Some of them are even married to each other. Then they have children and they grow up and work here as well. A bit like Dr Metcalfe, whose father worked here. He had thick bushy eyebrows, and a deep voice. I remember that.

I know all of this stuff about the ward meeting because me, Mike and Sid don't go anywhere on a Wednesday morning. Well, we do, we go to make the beds on Ward Eighteen, but that doesn't take all day.

By the way, if you ever come to Threeways and want to use the toilet, my advice is that it is best to go before a mealtime. If you wait until after, you will queue. Then when you get there, you will have to sit on a pan streaked with shit and listen to the grunting from the adjoining cubicle. I know that isn't nice to read, but it's worse to do, believe me. Hygiene is not high on the agenda here. When we have a bath, for instance, there are no locks on the doors. Now, that doesn't trouble a lot of us. We are used to lack of privacy, but it does worry newer patients. It isn't as bad as previously, when the nurses used to run one bath for nearly the entire ward. They weren't supposed to, but hot water was limited in any one morning. I was always so glad that my surname starts with a *C*. They would expect you to be in and out of that water in under five minutes, all to do with efficiency and routines. It was a sheep dip. You dared not delay, or they would prod you and tell you to get on with it. Of course, they had to occasionally top up the water that spilled over the sides, but it was generally cold by then.

There was a period when I played a game with the nurses, deliberately provoking them, but it got too easy. I learnt to prepare differently over the years. Now, I am able to pick my times. It is civilised compared to then. Mind you, the plug holes in the bathrooms are still all matted up with hair, and the soap looks desiccated. Never mind, grateful for small mercies, they say.

### *(For Martin)*

*There's a noise inside,*
*A flickering pain,*
*Red flashes of light,*
*Through the glass wall of fear.*

# Chapter Six

With a little luck, mealtimes pass by without incident but as often as not, they don't. A dispute frequently breaks out for the most trivial of reasons. Someone might have taken too much butter, or not passed the sugar, and a minor fight occurs, and the patients get untangled by the staff.

I am reading my Larkin book of poetry. A half-dressed patient is sitting crouched over an ashtray, grumbling to himself. His rambling is mixed with spontaneous bursts of laughter. Nobody cares; nobody takes any notice. Well, not the patients, anyway. A nurse finally tells him to go back to the dorm and put on a top.

I am sitting with Sid. His beard looks like a grey candy floss. It is resting on the table. If the cigarette were not clasped between his lips, his beard would resemble a rain-filled cloud. He has more hair on his chin than his head.

Me and Sid usually sit together at mealtimes. In fact, most of the patients always sit in the same place for their meals. Ray Thomas is the worst. He gets upset and cries if anyone is in his seat, which is surprising because he is the size of a haystack. I can tell when he's upset because his eyes fill with wet. (That sounds like a line for one of my poems.) His hands shake because he is trying to hold in the emotion. The nurses have given up asking why he wants the same chair every time.

They can't be bothered now and accept his ways. That happens over time. Ray has been here almost as long as me, and he is very particular about everything. He can tell you exactly how many days he has been in Threeways. He can remember facts and figures with no problem at all. He makes a mental note of the food at each sitting, something on which he will often comment later in the day. It normally concerns the number of potatoes he had, or the taste of the meat, or the quality of the dessert. I don't know how it started, but it has become such a thing on the ward that the nurses construct their conversation with him based around the meals of the day.

I know it is nice to have familiar things and routine, but sometimes I wish that we could get something different. Breakfast of Frosties, or some Bovril or even Shredded Wheat would be nice. I would be happy with any of the other breakfast stuff that is advertised on the television. It would make a nice change. I mean, some of us have teeth. There are not many choices to make here.

Don't they think we deserve a change now and then? The slop they feed us is boring. It's worse than boring because it's not nice. I don't like soggy toast. And why can't they let us make our own? It is to do with safety, they will say. They don't want us doing it because they don't think we can. And it's a lot quicker and easier for you to lay it out through the hatch. It's more convenient, I understand that. Convenience and control.

Ray rubs his fat fingers together in excitement. His ruddy face beams.

'Off to the gardens today. Yeah!'

Not before he has had his little green pills that make him docile and his head go woolly.

Two staff stand behind the trolley and unlock it with their big bunch of keys. They put up the lid and while one of them recites the medicine from a patient's medicine sheet, the other gives out the pills or syrup, handing it to the patient by the trolley. Or, depending on how generous of spirit they are feeling (and this is rare, you probably have to be dying to get that privilege), take it to them. Some staff carry out the procedure mechanically, and I can see this as a mundane part of their shift. I do not think some of them know what the pills are meant to do. I do not think anyone knows that really. They say they do, but they don't. For most of the others, it is another symbol of their relationship of power over the patients. Like I always say, this place is all about controlling others.

I am still thinking about Ray and the gardens as I leave the ward. When I get outside, I see the sky is grey and brown. Like a dirty badger. There is no sunshine to cheer us, to help the gardens grow, to help Ray with his digging. At least the snow has gone. The gardeners here, I mean the real ones, not the patients, they keep all the flowerbeds and lawns and trees immaculate. If you didn't know better, you might think that Threeways was a country estate not a mental hospital. Actually, they call it a psychiatric hospital now. That got changed in a while ago, but it doesn't matter what you call it, people still know it is a mental hospital. Anyway, when would someone like me ever get to live in a country estate? Only here, we don't hunt grouse or chase foxes, and we don't have sherry on the terrace. We have people to help us dress, but the comparison only goes so far. I am prepared to bet that the nearest Lord doesn't get his mattress tipped up if he is sleepy from the night time drugs. I bet if he can't motivate himself to get up in the morning he does not get kicked up the arse. Then told to get into the day room or he will miss breakfast and medication.

Speaking of the gardens, in spite of it all, this is a place where the flowers still bloom and where the birds still sing. It always amazes me how respectful we are of all the flowers. If this were outside, you know, the real world outside, you would find people lopping off the tulips to take home and put in a vase, or nicking roses to start their own rose bush. Why don't we get credit for being respectful to the flowers?

I am used to finding patients in the grounds behaving in a way considered strange in the outside world. There is a young woman on a bench. She is shouting. Irrationality, they would call it. I wonder why she has been let out without a coat. She is wearing a thin, ragged green cardigan. Her outbursts are sporadic, accompanied by flying spittle. Then she starts laughing. She looks at me and says, 'I know when I'm mad.' She probably does. We all do. All of us except the nurses and the doctors. This particular route takes me one thousand one hundred and five steps. Don't ask me how long I have been counting paces because I cannot remember.

Anyway, it is bitter today, and the wind slices through you. When I pass one of the porters by what we still call the ballroom, he calls it a lazy wind. When I ask him why, he says that is because it can't be bothered to go around you, and so goes straight through instead. I quite like that.

The ballroom is a huge hall. Some staff call it the dance hall. Whatever it is called, it is massive. It has an arched ceiling with fancy plasterwork panelling. There are leaded windows all around with coloured glass. There is a viewing area, a bit like a balcony, which has various pillars. There is also a stage. In the time I have been here, we have had dances and concerts and masked balls and concerts. The hospital had its own band once upon a time, I just about remember it. I remember the swirling, hypnotic enjoyment of the dances where the music and the chatter and the laughter would create a happy mix. It was one of the few times you would hear laughter at Threeways. Now, we just have the New Year's Ball. When you sit in the ballroom, you can sometimes feel the heating vibrating under your feet. That is the boiler is trying to send heat to the distant parts of the hospital. We are allowed to mix with the female patients now though, whereas maybe twenty or thirty years ago they used to try and keep us apart. All the wards were either male or female back then. The locks were different too. Can you imagine that? What a strange idea. They also show films in the old ballroom. I am going to go to the next showing.

Sometimes I go to the Threeways patients' library. That is where I learn most of the stuff I know. My favourite books are one which is about art and another all about lives of famous composers. Right now though, I am heading for the social club. That's the patients' social club. We call it *Fags and Shags* on account of the exchange of cigarettes and sex. You will find that the moral standards existing in this place operate under a tidemark of questionable height. I am pretty sure that the staff club is similar, I have heard them talking about it. They think we don't listen, but we hear what they talk about, when they are dishing up the food, or handing out the pills. They must think that they exist in a bubble. I suppose it's because of all that time they spend in the office. Either that, or they forget we are there. They are not so different from us. They come here every day, they do the same thing, eat the same food, and smoke all day long. The only difference is that they get to leave the hospital at the end of each day and they get paid for being here.

So we know what they get up to in their social club. Half of the male nurses arrive into work smelling of alcohol. It isn't hard to work it out.

*Fags and Shags* is a prefab, left over from wartime. It is wooden, with a green paint smeared over the outside. The roof is flat and leaks in places. I make my way down the pathway, trying not to slip on the mud, and open the door to feel a rush of fetid air. The wooden floor is scarred with cigarette burns, scuff marks, coffee spills and saliva from drooling patients. I find myself wondering why they don't send the cleaners over to use their mop and bucket here, but when you think about it, you realise that they would be fighting a battle they could not possibly win. If you get close to the other patients, you can smell the nicotine on their clothes. Closer still and it seeps from the ends of their fingers.

A patient is stuffing a chocolate bar into her mouth. She is cramming so fast that her hand is almost disappearing, as if to remove the chance of it being stolen from her.

I see Mike waving at me from the back of the building. He has a cup by his left arm and he is leaning on the table smoking. I step inside. There is a girl sitting by the entrance, staring at the door, as if she is waiting for something. But she isn't, I can tell. She has temporary residence in a distant galaxy. It is a common sight around Threeways. Any mental hospital, I suppose. She may have had oral medication to subdue her. Or an injection. They are pretty popular now, I suspect because they are easy for the nursing staff to administer. I mean, what can a frail-looking girl like her do when she is being held down by two stocky men, with another aiming a dirty great needle at her bottom? I don't mean to suggest the needles are *actually* dirty, by the way, it's just a figure of speech. So, here she is, dressed in mismatched and ill-fitting clothing, unaware of the world around her. I am not sure whether to feel envious or sad.

## *DRUGS*

*The spikes of experience are rolled into rounded orbs by the addition of chemical invasion, infusing the brain cells and discouraging the nerve endings in ways that psychiatry hopes will cure, but in reality will simply dull the emotions.*

They love medication here. The doctors and nurses never think there might be something else that can help. The doctors get particularly excited about every new pill that comes along, as if it is a magic act. They get visited by the drug company people who give them all sorts of free things. When they give us the drugs, they are mostly thinking about keeping us quiet. I know they talk about treatment, but the drugs they hand out do nothing except cause patients to get fat and slobber. They may as well scoop out our brains with a serving spoon. Plus, giving us pills makes them feel like they are actually doing something, as if talking to us will achieve nothing. We end up simply having a rear end like a dartboard, or acting as chlorpromazine slot machines, where the medication is fed in with no idea of the result but in hope of a jackpot. By the way, if you do not respond to the medication, they give you more, thinking that it is only a matter of dosages. That's a pretty stupid logic, if you ask me. There was a time when they had the fancy new medicines when they talked about curing psychotic patients. They don't really talk about cure any more. At least they have realised that much.

Another patient is demanding to know why helicopters have been flying over the hospital. Then he wants to know why his doctor is making the staff take his photograph without his permission. He mutters something about secret files and blacklists. He changes emphasis. 'And I don't care if he was in the infantry, he doesn't have the right to give drugs to a child.'

Of course it doesn't make sense. It is not supposed to. Then he moves on to start shouting about aliens. We get a lot of that. It's normal loony stuff. I suppose it keeps the public happy when they see a stereotype of madness. I like to think it is our way of reassuring the world by maintaining social order. You can never know what starts these thoughts. In this instance, though, I blame the Apollo space project. I watched it on a television in the day room when they landed on the moon. Well, they say they did. Funny thing is, if you listen to the nurses around here, you would think that half of the patients have already been there. They love a good conspiracy; it reminds me of that nonsense the nurses sprout about the full moon.

Anyway, Mike is still waving at me, so I get my coffee and go over to him. He has his tobacco spread in front of him like he's counting his winnings.

'Where's Sid?'

'Back on the ward,' I tell him. 'He's getting fed up.'

'Again? That's a shame,' says Mike. 'He was like that not so long ago.'

He is right, it wasn't that long ago that Sid was having to be coaxed out of bed. That is how bad his depression was. Sid says it's like having your body filled with wet sand. I feel sorry for Sid when he is like that, but at least he doesn't have to face the other problems at the Box Shop when he is unwell. Life has its way of occasionally presenting a small bonus. I warm my hands on the mug and sense movement beside me.

'I can see into space.'

An alien chaser has made his way to our table and is speaking in a deliberate, whispering tone.

'I see the Cosmos, the rays, the lights…'

'Looks like the drugs are working a little too well,' says Mike, as he leans in towards me.

We are used to patients hallucinating. It causes us so much less anxiety than it does the staff. They rush about, writing reports on every little movement made by their supposed psychotic charges. It provides them with purpose, I suppose, and things to talk about at their handover meetings in their office. And, of course, that builds into something that Dr Metcalfe can get his teeth into on a Wednesday. 'I'll change the pills', he will say. 'Start him/her on something new'. Yes, ha ha, something else that doesn't work.

They may be well-intentioned, but the psychiatrists get lost in a fog of their own theorising. What they can't understand, they attack with medication. I think the strangeness scares them, and so they try and make us fit into their idea of normality. Psychiatry is all about controlling others.

'Anyway, Sid…' Mike is staring at me, and his brown eyes are intense. I have never really noticed before now. Sorry, Mike.

'Yes, I'm worried that soon he's going to start talking about dying.'

By saying that, I don't mean the type of dying when a person thinks they are dying inside, like their lungs are deflating, or their ribs are breaking up. I mean a real feeling of impending death. That is what Sid gets like. I cough and it feels like gravel in my throat.

'Do you think it's because of the Box Shop?' Mike blows on his coffee.

'Could be. Williams is pretty rough on him.'

Mike nods. I know he is thinking the same as me. Why can't we help Sid, why can't we stop Williams being so mean? I know I said before that it is part of life in Threeways, but I really don't like it. Especially recently. It seems to affect me more as time passes.

'Why don't we report him?'

I scratch my head while I think about Mike's question. 'No, that won't work. Williams would lie. When do they ever believe us over a member of staff?'

'Well,' says Mike, in his stuttering tone, 'he's not going to suddenly turn into a nice person.'

Our pessimism is rooted in reality.

I almost tell Mike about Ron's project, but in the circumstances, I do not want to worry him. The thought enters my head that if I were to move, I would be free of Williams.

I start coughing. I have to go outside to spit the phlegm from my cough down to path by the side of the club. I strike a match and light another cigarette to calm my lungs. The bitterness hits the back of my throat and I cough again. Eventually, I catch my breath and look at the main building opposite. Already, a comforting yellow light is shining from the small windows on the chronics' ward. The day is so gloomy that the only light in the sky is already fading to the west. The building to my right is the alcoholic ward. It is a separate building. They call it a villa, but that isn't what I would call it. Back along, it was an isolation ward. We used to have outbreaks of TB from time to time. I am pretty certain that there was a cholera epidemic once, as well. Now it houses the drunks. I see them sneaking back into the grounds from the Star. The Star is the nearest pub. They aren't allowed out, but they go there instead of attending OT. They always find a way, and then they arrive back, stinking of booze with their bloodshot eyes and dishevelled clothing. Funny, though, because they also have a football team in a local league. I don't know how they manage that when they're full of either alcohol or drugs. Or both.

Mike arrives outside with my coat.

'Thought you might need this.'

He is right. I realise that I have been stamping my feet and rubbing my hands together to keep them warm.

'We had better get back,' I tell him. He agrees and we set off for the ward.

It appears that we have a new man in the day room. He is restless, pacing about like a man waiting for his wife to give birth. When he starts to shout, I know the show is about to begin. There is the special magic in these moments that makes a nurse appear from nowhere.

I watch the nurse. She edges towards the patient. She is holding her hands up in a gesture intended to suggest that she isn't a threat. Well, what do you think? He sees it as submissive, so he shouts louder. I can't make out what he is saying, exactly, but I can tell he is pissed off. He then starts banging his fists on the metal shutters that cover the service hatch to the kitchen. It really is a good way to grab their attention. Sure enough, another nurse appears. This one is male. Does he honestly think that saying 'Calm down' is going to work? I almost laugh out loud. He approaches the patient who pushes him in the chest. It isn't a violent gesture, he is defending his space. Well, I can see that, why can't they?

I don't have chance to consider the matter, because others arrive to grab an arm or a leg, both sets of which are now flailing about like an out of control Catherine wheel. The grappling continues for several minutes. I also see some punching that they try to hide. They take these things too personally, as if the man is being aggressive for the sake of it. The thing is, they don't know what it's like to be pushed about, told what to

63

do. They don't realise that it can be scary to be ordered about when you feel distressed.

Although I feel for him, I can't help thinking that such incidents keep the place going. It is like fuel, feeding the appetite of the organism, maintaining the energy. A surge of adrenalin is released in all of us. It provides the nurses with a reason to write in their reports, and then to share in their handover meetings. In there is also a reason for ward round, for prescribing medication, for the continuation of purpose. Everyone from the psychiatrist to the hospital porter can breathe more easily thanks to incidents like this.

The commotion settles down when the new man inevitably surrenders to the irresistible forces of the mental hospital. He is led away to a side room to cool off. Psychiatry is all about control. They will always win in the end.

Do you know what? It turns out that the patient was only after a cup of tea.

I turn away from the sideshow to see that Ray is sitting on the edge of one of the chairs with a big grin on his face. You might call it beaming. I can see that he wants to tell me about his day.

'Been to the gardens today, Tim,' he says. 'Snipped some bushes.' He is miming the action of pruning with both of his huge hands. They look like they could clear snow in a blizzard. 'Cleared up the leaves into the bags. Yeah. Fabulous.'

I can't help but comment.

'Wasn't it cold, Ray?'

'Naaah. Bloody fabulous.'

There is something comforting in his happiness.

We hear a shout from the kitchen. It is supper time.

## Beyond

*Beyond the white carpet of clouds, we fly like angels.*
*Beyond the stars, you can see forever.*

# Chapter Seven

I knew it was going to be a bad day when the banging woke me up. I thought it was content of my dream at first. Like the moon had swept down to earth and was threatening to carry us all away in our sleep. We would leave with our heavy heads and our over-medicated souls. In fact, I was dreaming of wartime and tanks and bombing raids. I think it was the war film we watched on the television. But it wasn't a dream. I woke up to see the blue overalls on a stepladder, hammering away at the pipes. When I saw my breath in the dormitory air that was when I realised how cold it was.

It snowed again last night. I thought it had gone for the year, but a blue glow is shining through the windows. I don't want to get up, because if the maintenance people are here and the heating is not working, then you can bet that there is no hot water. Shaving is going to be hard work. I stay inside the remains of the night-time warmth for as long as I can. Like a squirrel.

I was right about the shaving. When I arrive in the day room for breakfast, my face resembles the battleground on that war film. I hear the rattling of the food delivery. The tins are being stacked in the kitchen. Sid looks fed up. We can't be bothered to talk about the cold weather. Mike is wrapped up. He already has his coat on.

'All ready?'

I look up to see Jan. Jan is another nurse who works on my ward. She has been at Threeways a long time too. She has a niece who works in the hospital. Her niece is Ron's girlfriend.

'Good lads,' says Jan. She pats my arm. 'I know I can always rely on you, Tim. You're a gem'

She always calls me that. I know what she means, she means I never complain about going to IT. I should. But I don't.

'See you later, then,' says Jan. 'Ravioli for lunch today.'

Ravioli? Yuk.


The day doesn't improve when we get to the Box Shop. Outside the building there are icicles hanging from the roof. It might snow again later. I don't want to take my coat off when I get inside, but I have no choice. At least I put on a cardigan under my jacket. I now wish I had some gloves. That probably wouldn't be allowed. Williams is strict on anything that interferes with productivity. Talking of Williams, his mood is no different than usual. He is staring at us as we file in. He is a scowling, sneering foreman. As I get to my bench, I watch him, I can feel the blood pumping around my head. I know what is to come. I look over at Sid, who has his cardboard in front of him. I would rather we were in another place, but this is where we get sent.

The murmur of lighting and the rustle of production settles into its monotonous rhythm. The occasional cough pierces the tone. I think I hear humming, but it is so low-level that I cannot be sure. It might be in my head. I concentrate on the folds, left side up to meet front side; right side followed by back. I am folded, just like the cardboard in front of me. I am folded into the fabric of Threeways. As I think about this, I tuck the fold over to secure my first box. There is a rush of winter air from the door as a patient arrives late.

'Hurry up, you moron. You're late.'

The patient exclaims an apology, hangs her coat and scuttles to her bench.

'You're lucky we don't have cages any more, or I'd make you stay in one all day.'

Williams cackles at his own imagery. His shoulders rise and fall as he considers the idea. I do not think we ever had cages here at Threeways, so I imagine he may be referring to another place. Perhaps he worked at another asylum where they treated the patients like zoo animals. I doubt it, though. I think Williams is exaggerating in order to scare us. He likes to do that. It is all part of his game of cruelty.

He is eventually satisfied that there will be no more interruptions, but the latecomer seems to be the catalyst for Williams to start. He walks into the centre of the room, his cigarette stuck to his lip, one eye closed to keep out the smoke. He has his arms behind his back, prowling, looking for a victim. I watch him. I sense the blood in my head again as he bends his body forwards.

'You fucking imbecile.'

He gets so close that some spit hits Sid on the cheek. Williams' hands are shaking and I can't work out whether it is the fury or the drink. I wish for a moment that I knew where the special doorway was, because I would take Sid with me and out of here.

I don't think I said, but it is Sid's little finger that got torn off by the machine when he worked in the car factory. I may have said that. I can't always remember. It doesn't make any difference to his ability to pack the boxes up, but I suppose Williams somehow thinks it does. Like I said, it is one of the reasons he picks on him.

Williams makes a circuit of the department benches. He now had a steaming cup of tea in his right hand and this time he approaches Mike. Mike can sense Williams behind him and does not dare raise his eyes. I am watching, though, fearful for the next move. Williams stops, his face a mask of spite. His balding head shines as it reflects the weak light of the strip light. The split veins in his nose radiate out to his cheeks, themselves a shade of mauve. His mouth edges into a sadistic smile. Mike must be holding his breath as he wonders what Williams's next move will be. Williams slurps his tea and steps a pace closer to Mike. He leans in so that he is beside Mike's ear.

'And as for you, I can only imagine the fucking noise you make with that stupid guitar...'

I fear an assault. The pain in my chest feels like it has been made with a blowtorch. It gets worse at times like this. Luckily, Williams wanders off and I see Mike breathe out.

I do the same but my cough is bad this morning and I start spluttering in my efforts to suppress the noise. It is a funny thing, but I don't seem to draw the attention of Williams. If it were some other patient, I am pretty sure he would be telling them to shut up. I look at my watch and it tells me eleven o'clock. Ninety minutes until we escape, I hope Sid can hold out. There is a patient opposite me who packs about three boxes every ten minutes. That is not a very good rate. He stares at the cardboard every time, as if has to work out the procedure all over again. He doesn't let it bother him, he stares, his tongue pops out with the concentration, he scratches his greasy head. Then he smiles to himself, as if he has discovered the Holy Grail. All the while, he taps a forefinger on the cardboard. When he begins, he starts to fold the cardboard. When he is folding, he is deliberate, and he hums ever so faintly, but not so much that Williams can hear. It is lucky for him that Williams is partially deaf in his left ear. And in a constant state of minor drunkenness from his brandy.

It might be the sweat on his hands that makes Sid fumble. Williams starts a new wave of insults.

Midway through the morning, the patient pauses, as if he has had enough. I tell him to carry on.

'Don't stop,' I whisper. The patient looks at me and waves. He presents an innocent smile. He seems to understand because the humming starts again as he drags across a new template for his next box. I am relieved when I see him start up again.

My attention gets refocused when Williams appears for a new round of insults.

'Idiot. You're an idiot, do you know that? An imbecile, that's what you are.' There is a slap to the back of Sid's head. 'You can't even do the simplest task that we set you. No wonder you're in here. You're pathetic and weak.'

I watch as Williams raises his leg and kicks Sid in the calf with his instep. Sid puts his head down. He has learnt not to react. Sid doesn't dare raise his eyes. Williams is behind him and Sid seems to be holding his breath, wondering what Williams' next move will be. Williams slurps his coffee and steps closer to my friend. He leans in so that he is beside his ear. He flicks the ash from his cigarette on to Sid's head.

'You are a useless loon.'

Although Williams wanders off, I know he will be back. So does Sid. My pulse is surging and I have a pain in my chest. Watching the torture makes me feel ill. Every time we are here now, I wish Williams would die. I don't care how. He could have a heart attack, or a stroke, I don't care. I lie in bed worrying, thinking of how I can get rid of him. I have seen a lot of bad things here, and I am sad that it is still happening, if on a lesser scale. I wonder whether I should cause a distraction, or make a fuss so that Sid gets a rest for a day.

Sid looks at me from under his brow and I do my best to look supportive. Occasionally time can be like fudge. I know I said that time in Threeways passes in a blur, but that is not the case in this department. Here, time is held back as if by an unseen energy, a force pulling on the morning. I force the clock round with willpower.

# Chapter Eight

There are those who try to get close to our world, but their understanding collapses as it approaches our darkness. Ron tries hard to achieve the nirvana of all mental nurses, but he offers what he thinks are solutions when they are merely temporary sticking plasters. I think I have suggested that hope is an abandoned concept in this place. I get the feeling that Ron thinks he can help its resurrection. He took me to town today, out with the otherworlders. I felt guilty about missing the Box Shop and leaving Sid alone to face Williams. I hope it wasn't too unbearable for him. One consolation was that the weather was kinder today. Despite an early frost that was rock hard out on the lawns, the sun came out and it was almost springtime. I love the spring. It is my favourite season.

I got the impression Ron thinks I am stupid. Or, at least, incapable. I know I have been in Threeways a long time, it is getting on for forty years now, but I still remember how to buy things. In any case, what does he think we do with those ridiculous tokens they hand out at the Box Shop? Apart from which, the best currency in Threeways is cigarettes and tobacco. He probably doesn't realise the trades, particularly swapping fags for sexual favour. Some of the female patients will do anything for a fag. It might be a blow job, or full sex, it depends on how hard you barter. I must admit I have been involved in the trade from time to time.

I shouldn't complain about Ron. It was kind of him to think of me. The outside world is another place, though, and I can take it or leave it. Like I say, you can get fixed in a place like Threeways.

What would happen if I left, anyway? I worry about what would happen to Sid and Mike. And I would worry about Millie. Millie is my on and off girlfriend. She depends on me. She would miss me.

Before we left, Ron had to ask the head nurse if it was okay. I stood in the hall but I could still hear the two of them in the office.

'But he needs to do things like this if he is to progress.'

The head nurse asked Ron why he was bothering.

'If I'm going to be any good at being rehab coordinator for this ward, I need a success. I need to prove to the likes of Metcalfe that patients can manage.'

'I still don't get it,' said the head nurse. 'Why can't they just leave things as they are?'

Ron started talking about new ways of caring for people, as if Threeways would be closed down in a week or two. I know that is not going to happen. But I suppose things do eventually change. Too late for me, I think.

'Why Tim, though?'

This aroused my interest. I was possibly going to hear something about myself.

'If I can prove a long-term patient can make it, especially one who has been here for thirty years, then it will set a benchmark for the others.' A back-handed compliment. Not exactly what I had expected. 'And he's a nice guy. Why shouldn't he have a chance?'

That was better.

There was a pause. Ron poked his head back out from the office. He beckoned towards him. 'Tim, get over here.'

I walked forwards and stood at his side by the door to the staff office.

'Tell us why you want to go into town.'

Ron must have forgotten that he was the one that suggested the trip. 'To get a new record,' I said.

'He *wants* to buy a record. He wants to practice shopping, don't you, Tim?'

'Er. Yes. I suppose I do.'

'See,' said Ron.

He scratched his head and breathed out slowly. The head nurse, not Ron.

'You'll need to keep an eye of him,' he said, looking at Ron and not at me.

It is a strange thing, but the nurses here think we are fine as long as we are watched over through noon and night. They are obsessed with note-taking, I think I might have said that already. But more than that, they are terrified that the next unpredictable episode is waiting in the sidelines of eccentricity and unreason. Anyway, eventually the head nurse agreed and me and Ron set off to town.

We went to buy some jeans for Ron. There were some strange fashions in there, and curious music. The music is probably why Ron likes it there. I bought some presents for my friends and Ron was impressed. I was only being thoughtful. Does he think a mental patient can't be thoughtful?

When we were walking down the high street, I had to resist the urge to pick up a still burning cigarette that someone discarded on their way into the bank. I bent down and had to turn the movement into pretending to tie my lace. Good job I was wearing the brogues. It seemed such a shame to leave the butt, burning away neglected and so lonely. Another dog-end bites the dust. Did you know that the French word for dog-end is *megot*? No, I don't suppose you did. Don't ask me how I know that, I just do.

I enjoyed going to the record shop. It was full of posters and booths where you can listen to discs. Like your own private music group for one. That would be fun, but I would miss hearing Marjorie swear, and Neil spill his coffee all over his trousers.

Music is a thing that me and Ron have in common. Which is nice to be able to say, I think. After that, we went to a café and had iced buns and coffee. I bought a new record for Sid. He likes music. It is one of the few things he does like. Ron thought that was kind of me. I am neutral about that.

He stirred his tea for a long time, staring at the whirlpool he was creating. Then he suddenly asked me about getting out.

I was confused. 'Getting out?'

'Yes,' he said. 'Out of Threeways.'

He must have been feeling confident that having got me out to town, his plan would be easier to sell. I looked at the surrounding of the tea shop and told him I already was. I knew what he meant. I was just playing with him. Perhaps that contributed to him thinking I am a bit slow.

'No,' he said. His voice betrayed a hint of exasperation. 'Out for good. You know, the project I am in charge of on the ward.'

'Oh no, they would never let me out of there, Ron.'

'Why not?'

'They just won't.'

'Why not?'

The conversation was going to take forever if he was going to adopt a stupid approach as well.

'Where would they put me?' I said. 'Threeways is my home.'

It was all I could think of as a response. I wanted to say *What about Mike and Sid?* I could have added Millie's name. I also almost said that I would miss Jan. I like Jan. Before I said anything, Ron started talking again.

'There are some rehabilitation places in the town,' he said.

I still do not know what these are, but they don't sound like fun. All of a sudden I had a coughing fit. Pieces of bun got splattered over the table, and some coffee went up my nose, which made things worse. I went outside into the street and continued coughing. I saw my reflection in the teashop window and my face was red. Then I saw through the window, and inside the café, Ron looked worried. He was about to get up, so I held up a hand to tell him I was okay. The coughing subsided and I went back in.

After he asked me if I was okay for about the twentieth time, he said, 'So, what do you think?'

I had forgotten what he was talking about and must have stared at him with a confused expression.

'The rehabilitation? I'm the ward lead for the project. You would go to Linnet House first. You know, as a sort of stepping stone.'

'Oh,' I said, not really wanting to talk about it anymore. 'No. I'm stuck there, Ron.' I asked for another cup of coffee and that seemed to end that topic conversation for the time being.

When he came back, he asked me about my family. I never think about them, I told him. Then a thought occurred to me.

'I suppose I'm here because of my dad,' I said to him. I wished straight away that I had not said it, because he was suddenly very interested. All I meant was that it was the fights we had when I was a teenager that resulted in being taken to Threeways. Nothing more. I don't feel any emotion about the fact one way or another. I know I committed no crime, as such, and I am not a dangerous person, not by a long chalk. When I do think back to that time, pretty much all I can remember is that I was here in Threeways before I knew what's happening.

When I first arrived, they regarded me as dangerous. I was another insane young man, in need of correction. The place really was a madhouse then, one nurse to thirty or more patients, all behaving like they thought a mad person should. No wonder they used restraints. They were probably shit scared.

They tried all kinds of silly stuff back then, all called therapy, of course. All in the name of treatment. Insulin shock, that was one of them. They gave you insulin until you passed into a coma, then they revived you out of it, or something like that. What were they hoping to do? Shock me back to being normal? You can't shock a person to feeling better, otherwise all the psychiatrist would need to do is jump out from behind a tree. It is the same with the electroshock, the ECT. Why they think that will cure a person with mental suffering is beyond me. At least I missed the teeth extraction and appendix removing period. That was where they were so desperate to find a cure that they chopped out the bits they thought were septic. I also avoided the brain surgery. Not like my old friend Walter. He was never the same and he died not long after they chopped out part of his brain, thinking it would cure him. He never got to see past 1961.

Of course, now they give us pills that make your head fuzzy, your body pile on weight, and your mouth dry. Then they give us more pills to counteract the unwanted side effects. What logic.

Sorry, I got sidetracked, I meant to tell you about Ron. I like him, but he is idealistic. He gets wrapped up in his own dreams. I mean, his idea for getting people out of Threeways; it is well-intentioned, but how do you shift someone like me, who knows little else?

He is right to ask about why I am here, but not in the way he thinks. I know I should not still be here in this place, but here I am. One day I will tell him about the diagnosis of schizophrenia that led to the incarceration, the manhandling and the mind messing they have done in a flurry of thioridazine and hand slapping. I'll tell him about arguing my case against the medical establishment that it made me look madder. I don't have a voice, and if I do, they either don't listen or treat me badly me for being a troublemaker. You can't win.

What I do know is that my life counts for little, it passes in the sizzle of a sausage or the trill of a whistle. At the end of it all I will get returned to the endless eternity of space. It makes you wonder what the point is.

Still, I cannot help but admire Ron's optimism. At least there's a bright spot in the hospital. Not all the nurses are lazy or cruel, like you might think. You have to remember that they get bored as well, and they have to put up with getting beaten themselves, at times. It is really no surprise that they get detached from themselves and the relationships they should have with the patients. Us and them, that is what they see, some of them. Ron is not like that. He wants to present another way, but the surroundings here envelop you, there are forces that cause you to stumble inside a life that should offer more.

Ron handed me another cigarette and we smoked together like a couple of friends while we waiting for the bus back to Threeways.

We got back and walked the three hundred and two steps up the driveway. That is how many it was today. Sometimes it is more, but Ron was walking with a long stride. Ron disappeared into pharmacy and I carried on alone. As I approached the main block, the slate tiles of the roof were glistening with wet from the rain. There was a rainbow behind the building. They say that there is gold at the end of a rainbow. I started to think about the song that was sung by Judy Garland. Perhaps that's what Ron feels about trying to move me out of Threeways.

Harold Arlen wrote that tune. I know that thanks to Ron and his music. The Great American Songbook: Gershwin, Johnny Mercer, Cole Porter, Irving Berlin. Ron played them in a group once. Edward loved it all. After the group, he told me about lots of the composers and song writers.

The moon was out by the time we arrived. A full moon. And you know what? PL was wrong: it doesn't hurt the eyes. It does the opposite.

I pushed the door and went in. I walked down the main corridor and noticed that the old man who I think looks for the secret doorway was not there. Perhaps he finally found it, his doorway. I hope so, I would like to think he escaped to a better place. Sadly, he probably just died.

**(Dedicated to the man in the corridor)**

*Alone with his thoughts.*
*He looks for that door.*

*This way then that*
*Wandering the floor.*

*But today, the he is gone*
*His presence no more.*

# Chapter Nine

Here's a story I wrote that was inspired by my friend Sid. It's called *Professor Parker's Beard*.

His students at Budapest University talk about it. Professor Parker's beard hangs around his chin like a grey cloud of candy floss.

'Only, if you squeeze it,' says the one, 'it wouldn't compress into a sticky mess. Or maybe it would.'

'It must be two feet long,' says another.

'He looks like Santa Claus.'

'No,' says the other, 'more like Darwin.'

'Yes, it's weird.'

'It's hard to know where the mouth is.'

During lectures, they watch as the words emerge fully formed through the tangle of hair.

'It has an ecosystem,' says the student to his friend.

'Yes, you can probably find lost treasures of the Habsburgs there.'

The two of them laugh, when they really should be listening to what Wittgenstein has to say about language being ultimately meaningless. This is ironic, because if they *were* listening…

Words eventually stop emerging from Professor Parker's beard, and the students understand that it is time to move on to their next lecture. The work assignment will prove difficult for the distracted two. They will soon realise that they will have to ask their cohorts for a copy of their lecture notes. The lecture room clears in a flurry of capes and squeaking shoes.

The following day, Professor Parker wakes late. He yawns and stretches. His body creaks with age, his joints feel like reluctant gate hinges. He looks at the shaft of sunlight peeking through the crack in the thin curtain, welcoming him to an optimistic new day. He stumbles through to the bathroom. His critical faculties are subdued, like he has been sedated. Instead of the usual mental table tennis, his head is full of rocks. His mouth is filled with sawdust. Professor Parker realises that he does not feel well, he has a fever. His back aches, his skin is tender. His scalp is aflame.

It is clear that he will not undertake his usual Saturday morning rituals. He will not walk to the town centre to buy a newspaper and pipe tobacco. He will not sit in the park and watch the ducks. He will not go to the corner café for coffee at eleven o'clock. And so, after urinating, he returns to bed. As he shuts his eyes, he feels the throbbing behind the heavy lids.

Beard has already decided to have a proper day off...

They describe a grey cloud...But grey clouds generally represent portentousness: looming bad weather, bad news. Beard feels alive, vibrant, exhilarated.

Outside and independent, Beard is impressed with the ability to perceive. *How fresh. How bright the world is.* People stare, but why would they not? After all, it is an unusual sight. The self-awareness is refreshing. *The freedom is exhilarating. I can't believe I am stuck with that stuffy old professor all day long.* Knowledge of one's own awareness. *Who was that?*

Beard tries to recall the person who came up with the idea of ridding presuppositions. *Husserl. That was it. Not so long ago. I should know that. I tell all those eager faces in the lecture halls.*

Feeling pleased with the notion of being, Beard leaves the house.

*Heidegger. He was another one. If I ever meet that man, I will tell him that for all his confusing words, it is in being that we get our salvation.*

Professor Parker remains in bed. He rolls about in the sweat-soaked sheets. Weekends offer a respite from academic demands, a chance to pursue more leisurely activity. His fondness for hiking is cleansing. Intellectual respite is welcome. In reality, he experiences little of the bitterness of everyday folk, enjoying as he does the status and privilege of university life.

Beard passes the shops: tailor, hatters, merchants. Often they are run by immigrant Germans. After passing through some of the alleyways and stinking streets, Beard decides to make a visit to the National Museum. He can take time to appreciate those things that present themselves to him like they would not to others. It will be good to see the beards of great forebears like Rákóczi.

Inside the gallery, the halls are cavernous. Gilded cornice work up above, tiled elegance below. Polished marble everywhere in between.

After a while, Beard decides to rest on a bench seat and stare at the art.

*Why the professor has not brought me here, I will never know. He spends his weekends alone reading the newspaper and preparing for lectures. I should encourage him to get out more, to see the sights of Budapest. Rudas Baths, Vienna Gate Square, Gellért. They are all there for us to enjoy.*

Beard looks at the gathered crowd. Not really a crowd. More of a gaggle. They are admiring an enormous painting by Rafael. One of the group looks his way.

'I'm sure that is Professor Parker's beard...'

Although he whispers the words, Beard hears the pronouncement more clearly than ever. Having been recognised, Beard decides to leave. He moves through the oak doors and into the square. A statue of a man on horseback. Prince Eugene? *I should know this. I am part of a learned ensemble.*

Beard decides the matter is of minor importance. He laughs at the statuary on the Sàndor Palace. *Look at you all, solidified in time, unable to move. I am free.*

The exhilaration of liberty returns. He moves along until he reaches the Chain Bridge and passes over to Danube. The river looks dark, the water rushes past. Sunlight illuminates the parliament building in a golden hue.

Moving towards Pest, the river is less clear at the edges. There are bits of floating debris: used wrappers, pieces of cabbage, and old newspapers. There is even a glove gliding by. *What a disgusting situation. This city has become a dumping ground.*

Passing into the central district, Beard spies a nearby pub. After brief consideration, Beard decides the unnecessary dram would cause dizziness. *But that will not affect my thought process.* The decision to go inside is, on reflection, a good one. *My decision. Schopenhauer argued that things don't have free-will, but people do. That's what I tell the students when Professor Parker does his lectures. I should know, they are the words I speak for him.*

The landlord serves the drink. And then another. Beard takes a box of matches from the bar. No words are spoken.

*We are equal. Ràkosi and his merry band have created a form of peace beyond the tyranny of Uncle Joe.*

After leaving the pub, and feeling light from the vodka, Beard decides to test the theory of free will. His first attempt will be to push someone into the nearby canal. He waits on a bench, pretending to watch the birds in the sky. He has his attention focused on the passing pedestrians.

*Here's one. Homburg hat, long coat, creased leather shoes. Perfect.*

The man approaches, his chin is pushed into his coat against the chill air. Footsteps click their efficiency on the paved walkway.

Some thought has gone into the process. *I can lean*

*into him. Pretend I didn't see him coming. Then, nudge.*

Click, click. Closer.

Beard moves. And then stops. Freezes. The man walks on, without even tipping his hat in recognition.

*Why did I hesitate? A case of moral exactness? Fear? What did Rousseau say?* Man is in chains? *No, think more along the lines of Descartes,* I think so I am. *I am. I can act. I am.* I can.

The next subject, Beard decides, will not get off so lightly. He makes his way to another bridge. This one is in a dormant part of the city. It has a low handrail. A few walkers, a pram. Beard waits. A dog skips past. Finally, a subject. A young woman. She is wearing a fur coat. A red beret worn askance over copper hair. Vermillion lipstick.

*This time I will act with conviction.*

He moves forwards, timing the nudge to perfection. The woman topples, at first attempting to catch herself. An outstretched arm, a sideways shuffle. Those heels do her no favours. A high-pitched screech is her response to a further encouraging shove. Beard watches as she descends off a bridge into the inky water below. The sound reminds him of a rock hitting water. It is followed by splashing, like a child's bath time.

*She must act. For her own good. I do not know for certain the conclusion to this situation.* He thought about Kant, about knowing outcomes and the synthesis of reason. And yet, there is no *a priori* knowledge. All those lecture words resonate in the air. *I have spoken these theories over and over. Hundreds of students have listened to the wisdom. And*

90

*yet I cannot fathom the importance.*

Back in his bedroom, Professor Parker lies still. Hair is matted to his troubled brow. The muffled sounds from outside mix with the wind blowing under the window frame. A whistle from a ghoulish world.

Meanwhile, Beard has left the scene. He heard the spluttering behind him for some time after he departed. Now, a church lies ahead. Stone built, with Baroque embellishments. Not quite the gothic power of Mátyás, but an opportunity nonetheless.

*Confession. Is that what I should be doing?*

Although he has not experienced the scenario, Beard imagines what will happen. The priest will ask, 'What is it that I can help you with, my child?'

'I killed someone,' Beard will answer.

'That's a serious matter.' Beard will remain silent. 'How can you be sure you did this thing?'

'Because I watched her drowning.'

'And why? What thing was driving you to do this?'

'That's easy. It was an exercise in free-will, Father.'

'OK. Say some Hail Marys and repent.'

'That's it?' Beard will ask. 'I might have murdered a person and you let me leave with the promise to say a couple of repeated phrases?'

'Your conscience is with the Lord.'

*Religion! The worst thing to happen to mankind.*

Thoughts of the wars from the past, the brief foray by the Turks, the conversion of churches into mosques

by the Ottomans. The arrival and departure of Marie
Theresa.

*Religion is not the opium, Karl, it is the amphetamine of
conflict.*

His concerns return to his deed. *Is there moral code
for a beard? Will there be a Platonic injunction for my actions?*

But he will not see the stalls and the ornate carved
wooden pulpit, as Beard decides against the
confession, fearing it unwise. It would appear that the
only real sanctuary is to be discovered in the anonymity
of human shelter.

*They will pursue me, but how absurd to be looking for a
beard. Is not a beard something that one employs for a disguise?*

There are no sirens, no clanking bells, no whistles.

*Maybe the woman got out. She might have been saved.*

Beard hurries along, mingling with shoppers and
deciding that his crime would be lost in the annals of
time. He wondered whether the woman was a whore.
Would that make the crime less evil?

*That is rationalization, surely? Would Freud or perhaps
one of the other psychologists accuse me of receding into the depths
of self-doubt. Fenichel:* to justify irrational instincts as
reasonable. *That will do. It is rationality at its best. I will tell
the professor.*

The thought of the professor made Beard start to
worry. Was his day of liberty likely to ruin the
distinguished academic?

The hurry through the streets of Budapest began.
The outside was suddenly a fearful place, full of threat
and uncertainty. And what of the professor?

*He will ask*: Where have you been? *I will tell him that I have been out.* Oh, where, exactly? *I will tell him I have been collecting data for his lectures.*

The frantic dash back home has the effect of exhausting Beard.

By Sunday morning, the fever has lifted. The wind has died down. And Professor Parker wakes to find his beard under his nose once again.

# Chapter Ten

Sister Saunders has a pinched face like the scrunched-up crisp packet, and her hair is tied into a tight bun beneath her cap. She seems to think coldness is also efficiency. That doesn't make her bad, necessarily, just a bit too fond of her authority. She is another fixture, like me. There are a lot of these distant, stern women running wards in Threeways. She runs Ward Nine, which is in the east wing of the hospital. It is a female ward with twenty-five long-term patients. It is neat, despite the chaos of the inmates. They have tables with vases and pictures of landscapes on the walls. Well, it is their home, I suppose. That is what the nurses say sometimes. 'It's their home. Why shouldn't they have nice things?' They try and make the wards like their own homes. They will never succeed because they do not understand what it is really like to live in Threeways. That is not their fault, and I know they are only trying to improve things for the ladies here.

Sister Saunders has a no-nonsense approach to managing her ward. She is not unkind and I would not rate her low on the KQ scale, because her management policy is probably wise. Ward Nine is rowdy and full of mad women. I say full of mad women, but that is where Millie lives. I think I already told you that Millie is my on and off girlfriend.

I make sure I go to the office and say hello. It is all part of the cordiality that keeps me in favour. Sister

95

Saunders is writing in her daily report. I wave politely and tip my chin up in recognition, although I really feel that I ought to bow. Sister nods at me and just for a moment I think I make out a smile on her lips. It reminds me of an ECG pattern, irregular and uncertain. Anyway, I feel an unexpected but warming sense of approval spread in my chest. I wonder for a moment what she is like at home, away from the dominion of Threeways. She isn't married, I know that much. Perhaps she keeps a neat garden and has five cats to keep her company. She might be a totally different person away from the hospital. I would like to think she has that sensitive side to her. It balances a person; don't you think?

Millie is thin. She has a girlish giggle and she is younger than me. I go to visit her, but I am not always let in, I never know why. It is probably depending on who is playing up. Some of the women charge up and down the ward smoking, puffing relentlessly on a cigarette. Millie's standard is to giggle all the time. Marjorie is also on Ward Nine. She has a dolly on her bed. It makes me smile every time I see it. Sometimes I see Heather, a ginger-haired lady with a grumpy expression who says little and smokes a lot. There is another lady who drinks water as if she is expecting the pipes to be cut off. The ladies in Ward Nine are individuals. They are separate from one another and not a collective. They carry on their lives as if the others are not there. They fight a lot too.

Anyway, arriving at Ward Nine is like a game of chance—like it was today when I heard the key being rattled into the escutcheon—presenting myself here into a wave of excitement, a conditioned response they would call it, so that when I know I am being let in, I feel a heightening joy.

As far as I can tell, Millie seems to have three dresses. There is the blue one, with white stripes, the green one with poppies printed on it, and the black one. Today, she is wearing the green one; it is her favourite. It also happens to be mine. She has a blue shawl over her shoulders and she smiles when she sees me. Her emerald eyes are shiny; the shine escapes through her fine wrinkles on her eyelids.

I step forwards and offer a posy of flowers to Millie. It is nothing elaborate, just a few flowers I stole from the reception area that looked nice. I made sure nobody was watching. The reception is one of the few places where you can walk about unobserved. People in the main building are too busy walking about with files to notice another man in a jacket and tie.

Millie takes the flowers and holds them to her bony chest. You would think I had presented her with a diamond necklace.

'Shall we go to the social?' I ask. She probably wouldn't mind, but I don't call it *Fags and Shags* to Millie.

'You will need a coat,' I tell her. 'It's cold out.'

I watch Millie go to her dorm. She returns with her coat. 'I put my flowers in a cup of water.'

I take her hand and as we leave the ward and I notice a woman hitching up her skirt. A nurse is approaching with a look of concentration. It must be depot day.

We walk past the smoking chimney of the laundry, with its white smoke belching out. The blackened top is the only clue to the industry within, where the thousands of sheets and towels are processed every week. As we pass the block that contains the dentist (it is a few doors along from the mortuary, somewhere I will be one day), I think about all the teeth removed in the name of treatment. Like I said before, the search for madness back in the times when I arrived that they took out bits of patients' bodies to see if that was it. How did they ever imagine teeth could make you barmy? I mean, it's madness to think such a thing.

'How are you, Millie?'

She smiles at me and her cheekbones form into two little rosy apples.

'Is everything okay on the ward?' I ask.

'Marjorie got told off.'

Why doesn't that surprise me? 'What did she do?'

'Sister said she was smoking in the dorm.'

'Was she?'

'I'm not sure, but I heard Sister say, "You know smoking isn't allowed in the bedrooms, don't you?" It makes me laugh how Millie puts a bass tone in her voice when she imitates Sister Saunders. 'Marjorie said she wasn't doing it but Sister didn't believe her.'

'What happened then?'

'Well, I noticed there was a lot of smoke coming from her handbag.'

I laugh at this statement.

'Sister took her bag and said she wouldn't get any more cigarettes for the day.'

See what I mean? It is all about control.

I decide on a bland response. 'Well that's Marjorie, she doesn't learn.'

Mind you, there are lots of patients who test the nurses. It relieves the boredom. Can you imagine the monotony of existence here?

We pause for Millie to put on some lipstick that is not exactly contained to her lips, and we walk together, Millie and me, past the main kitchens. I can smell cabbage, even though it is cottage pie today, if I am not mistaken. I can hear the clanking and shouting of the work going on, the preparation of hundreds of meals ready to be loaded onto the delivery wagons.

We are stopped by a patient who wants a light. She is dressed in a blue dress with shiny white shoes that are too big for her. She doesn't say anything, she just holds out a cigarette and an inquisitive expression.

Millie isn't allowed a lighter. It is policy on Ward Nine. More control, see. I reach into my jacket pocket and flip open my lighter. The woman leans forward to greet the flame. I can smell her breath as she gets close and it is a sweet smell. She sucks greedily at the cigarette until a third of it is ash. It is like watching a cartoon. The woman also has a brown streak in her blonde hair. It reminds me of Robert. He was a man on my ward. He wasn't allowed a lighter either. One night, he removed the grille from a gas heater in an attempt to get a light from the flames for a butt he scrounged down at *Fags and Shags*. The problem was, he leaned a little too close and set his hair on fire. I laugh when I think of the nurses charging into the room to see what the smell was. Robert was reclining in an armchair.

'What's going on?' they demanded.

'I burnt my hand,' said Robert.

'How did you do that?' asked the nurses.

'Putting out the fire on my head,' said Robert, taking another puff from his butt.

That was funny. He didn't care, though.

'What you laughing at?' asks Millie.

I shake my head and smile, replacing the lighter into my jacket. He isn't here anymore. Robert, I mean. He once tried to shoot himself with a shotgun when his son died, but he didn't manage to kill himself. That is why he was here. In the end, I think the sadness took him. He was a nice bloke.

The woman in the oversized shoes is pleased to see the end of her cigarette glowing. She thanks me and wanders off. Her handbag is hanging from the crook of her arm, which is itself held aloft into the air.

Millie and me, we stroll down the incline past the entrance block. It strikes me that I have never really before noticed the arrogance of the clock tower sprouting from the building. I look at how it stands out as a phallic symbol, with the weather vane on top that seems to survey everything below like a metal Mr Williams. I wonder if the psychiatrists have ever analysed the sexual nature of our own architecture. I laugh again, and I notice that Millie has her head on one side and is starting to look at me strangely.

We stop off at the shelter in one of the airing courts for a breather. The wind is light and tugs at Millie's hair. I reach across and stroke her head. These shelters were a place where patients could huddle when we were kicked out of the wards during the day. The bench is cold and damp when we sit, the old wood sodden with the dank air creeping about the grounds. I can feel the wet seep into my trousers.

Millie has closed her eyes; she has a grin on her lips. I watch her breathing, which is rapid. I can almost feel the soft pounding of her heart within her chest. These are days that are worth living, days when it does not matter who is in charge or what I will do tomorrow. This is not a time to consider the future, and certainly not the past. Not that I know much about that. Like I told you before, it becomes a muddle of medication and madness.

I put my arm around Millie and I say nothing. I simply watch the scenery.

The clouds are fluffy, it makes a change from the dirty clouds of the past few days. No rain today.

I suddenly hear a voice calling my name. When I look up, I see Ron striding up the driveway. He is waving and heading in our direction.

I wave back. 'Hello, Ron.'

'Hello, Tim. Millie.'

Millie giggles.

Ron is out of breath. 'It's a long walk, that drive. I don't think I'll ever get used to it,' he says.

'Where have you been?'

'Linnet House.'

That's a name I heard him say when we went to town. At least, I think that was when. My memory is not so good as it was for things like that. I guess my expression tells him that.

'It's the new rehabilitation place. The old Lodge.'

Now I know. 'Oh, the Lodge. Why didn't you say that before? And now they call it?'

'Linnet House. It's the rehabilitation unit I was telling you about. It's only small, but it's a start. It's a staging post for people like you who might want to leave Threeways.'

A voice screeches beside me. 'You're leaving Threeways?'

He has dropped me in it.

'No Millie, it is just something Ron mentioned to me. I'm not leaving.' I have to put my arm around her for reassurance.

Ron combs his fingers through his long hair and inhales through gritted teeth. He can see he has caused a commotion in her little head. 'Sorry, I didn't mean, well, I just thought…'

I hold my hand up and change the subject. 'It's okay, Ron. Me and Millie are just off to the social. I'll see you later.'

He grimaces an apology, and we leave him sitting at the shelter. His expression seems to be wavering between uncertainty and regret.

'Are you leaving?' Millie asks me in a soft voice as we walk off.

I shake my head and smile at her, but I wonder about leaving more than I ever have.

## THE DEPOT

*It is the needle that causes quiet.*
*That hollow steel spike, aimed inaccurately at soft flesh,*
*delivers the potent oily mix to start*
*the journey from buttocks to brain.*
*The slow-release, time-lapsed, modern-designed, effective*
*method of control.*

# Chapter Eleven

You want to know what nothingness looks like? It is like an abandoned quarry, or an open grave just after the diggers have left. There are periods of extreme boredom here. The empty spaces are something that you get used to. You have to or you would go mad. Well, you know what I mean by that. In the end, you switch off, choosing instead to stare at a wall or watch a television programme without really watching it. And you work your way through a series of cigarettes. That's what most of the patients have learnt to do here. The pills can help, they give you a buzz, or make your brain go fuzzy. Makes up for the times when I cannot think straight. My brain gets like that from time to time: tangled in its own connections.

But no boredom today, because today is Wednesday and another ward round. When the door eventually releases them all back into the ward, the different professionals drift out their meeting. The nurses go to the office, the social workers stand about and chat, and then go off the ward. The head nurse calls the social workers the 'hand wringers'. I think he means that they worry too much. As opposed to him because he does not worry. That's what happens when you get used to Threeways, you stop worrying about the people inside it.

Dr Metcalfe is one of the last out, with the head nurse following, then Dr Cooper, who is our junior doctor. They look like ducklings following their mother. Dr Cooper is here for six months, learning about psychiatry. I always think they only need to let them spend a few nights in my dorm to learn that.

'Tim, can I have a quick word?'

It is Ron. His blue tie is in a neat knot, as always. I often watch him flattening his long hair in the mirror and retightening the knot, as if he is proud of it. He should be, it is an impressive knot.

'Of course,' I say. 'What is it?'

He beckons me to follow him and we go to the Blue Room. We sit down. Ron looks pleased with himself.

'Dr Metcalfe would like to see you,' he starts. 'But first he wants to see Dr Cooper.'

When I ask why, Ron starts telling me about Dr Cooper, which isn't what I meant. He says that Dr Cooper made a joke about ECT when they were talking about a patient, and he said they should 'Plug him in'. Ron hates ECT. I happen to know that, so he objected. Pretty brave, if you ask me. Anyway, Dr Cooper has to see Dr Metcalfe for a telling off, by the sound of it. I am not sure I want to be following Dr Cooper if Dr Metcalfe is in a bad mood.

'So why does he want to see me?' I ask Ron what I consider to be a valid question. As I have told you previously, they are never interested in me.

'Well.' Ron pauses and strokes his chin, trying to buy some time, I think, or create a look of thoughtfulness. I focus on the picture on the wall. It is a Constable. 'The thing is, Tim,' he says, 'Dr Metcalfe liked my idea.'

A cold wave passes down my body and back up my chest, which starts hurting. I start coughing again and hold my handkerchief over my mouth. Ron probably thinks I am trying to make him leave me alone. In a way, I suppose I am. The idea that I am the focus of his project is bad enough, but I don't want to go to Dr Metcalfe's office. It is like seeing the headmaster. Ron tells me not to worry, it will be all right, he says. Nothing to worry about at all. Really, don't worry.

Easy for him to say.

I see Dr Cooper leave and come through from the office. His face is red.

It is my turn. As I head towards the office, I see the sign: *Dr B Metcalfe MD MRCPsych*. I am approaching the executioner's axe. I am already on the gallows, having walked up the steps. Do they use gallows for beheadings? Or are they just for hanging people? I really don't know about that one. I seem to remember reading about the French and their guillotine. I think they used a gallows for that. Or perhaps they didn't. I also remember reading about Tyburn in London, where they would take the poor people condemned to death. I do not mean the poor people, like they have no money, only that I feel sorry for their destiny. Although they probably were not wealthy. I think the French were the only ones to do that to the wealthy.

My thoughts are an excuse to try and avoid the inevitable. I am finding it hard to control the trembling in my legs as I knock on the door.

'Come.'

That's it? One word. He didn't even ask who it was. I suppose he already knows.

I think about PL as I step through the door. In 'Next Please,' he says: *Always too eager for the future, we pick up bad habits of expectancy.* These sound like Ron's hopes that I do not currently share.

I look around at Dr Metcalfe's office. It has never struck me as interesting. The walls have the same sickly pale-green colour as the nurses' office. There are various notices on the walls, certificates and diplomas, pictures of himself with other people. Fellow psychiatrists, I am guessing.

Dr Metcalfe indicates for me to sit. He is sitting behind his desk. I can see his tweed suit beneath his white coat.

'Good morning, Tim.'

Well, a good start, he remembers my name.

I say hello. There is a wooden hat stand in the corner with his trilby hat, raincoat and a black umbrella stowed in it. To its left there is a set of screens by an examination couch, and a cream-coloured angle poised lamp fixed to the wall. Next to that is a small white sink. Sometimes the junior doctors use this office for medical examinations. This is where they test the reflexes of new patients with a rubber hammer. They also listen to heart rates or take blood here.

Dr Metcalfe goes to the metal filing cabinet in the corner and opens the middle drawer. He takes out a folder and places it on the desk. The file makes a thumping noise on the desk. It is a thick file.

I wait for him to continue, but he is sitting in his leather chair reading the notes. He starts annotating with his black fountain pen. He looks like a waxwork. His hair is thinning and swept back on his head. Dr Metcalfe has been at Threeways longer than most of his patients.

'Ron has been telling me about his plan,' he says eventually, looking up from the notes.

'Yes,' I say, 'he mentioned to me.'

I notice a picture of Dr Metcalfe standing by his car outside a building. I recognise it as the golf club opposite the hospital. He looks proud of his Jaguar. I wonder if he ever sees wandering patients on the golf course. I can imagine him striding along in his plus-fours, he could come straight out of a P G Wodehouse book.

'He is championing your cause,' he says.

I nod, not sure where the conversation is going.

'Well, what do you think of that?'

'You are the expert,' I say. To my ears it sounds like a terse response.

'No, Tim. I am a psychiatrist, looking after the welfare of the patients in a medical capacity. I am not one of these new social workers. I merely protect, you understand.'

I nearly laugh but manage not to. I think the word he is looking for is control.

'Now let's see.' I watch as he levers open the case notes. 'Yes. Problems at home, wasn't it.' He scratches his head. 'Well, you have certainly been with us a long time.' He should know that already. I knew his father.

'A lifetime,' I tell him.

'Yes.' He is staring down at the notes again, rubbing his finger along his lip in concentration. 'So what would you say to the chance of living outside Threeways? Given that you have been here so long.'

It sounds to me like a loaded question. I wonder if he is expecting me to say I want to stay, like Colin. About three years ago Colin was rediscovered by some relatives. They contacted the hospital, and, by the time they turned up, Colin had his future mapped out. I don't know how much choice he had in the matter, but I do recall that he was reluctant to leave. When the day arrived, he was dressed in pyjamas and refused to put on clothes. He disappeared from the ward and a couple of nurses were sent to find him. They discovered him over by the clock tower, trying to hide behind one of the buttressed walls of the main building. He ran when he saw them disappearing into the wooded area down by the cricket field, leaving one of his slippers in his wake as he fled. As he was running, he threatened them with the police and apparently shouted to anyone that would listen that he was being kidnapped. I seem to remember that it took most of the day to coax him out and on to the ward. His worried relatives must have been wondering about their decision.

I realise that Dr Metcalfe is waiting, and I am not sure how to respond. My silence seems to do the talking for me.

'You're an honest chap. Do you think you could manage outside the hospital?' he says. He is probing for a definitive no, I suspect.

'This place is my home,' I tell him. For the first time ever, it sounded strange. 'What I mean is, I have been here so long, I don't know any different.'

Now the opposite happens and Dr Metcalfe is staring at me.

'I mean; I didn't think I would ever be let out of here.'

'Because of...'

'Because of my past, I suppose.'

'Yes, I have refreshed my memory from your notes.'

What he means is, I had forgotten all about you and your past. Just like I have been trying to do all these years.

'The past goes back a long way,' I tell him.

'Well, a knife attack is a serious matter.'

It wasn't a knife attack. It was more of a misunderstanding. No good telling him that. I tried that all those years ago and nobody believed me then. Dad was happy to have me out of the way, as it happens. What would I have gone back to?

'I'm not like that, doctor.'

'So do you not think people deserve a chance?'

'Maybe…I never really thought about it.' And that is the truth, I have never thought about that.

'Well, that is what, it seems to me, young Ron is suggesting. It is certainly what he said in the meeting this morning. He spoke with some energy on the matter, in fact. Quite passionate, he was. It is not a subject that we usually consider, as you can imagine.'

I can imagine that without any difficulty. This is the most I have heard him say in all my time here. It is unusual. I consider how many other patients have this privilege. Not many, I bet.

'I should expect we will be getting more of this,' says Dr Metcalfe. 'I would like to know how you feel. As a sort of test case.'

'What do *you* think, doctor?'

'Me? Well,' he says, 'there are examples of long-term patients leaving hospitals. The movement to rehouse patients is gaining some momentum. The effectiveness of the latest medication is such that we are now able to cure a great many diseases of the mind, you understand.'

I am not aware of many people in Threeways being miraculously cured, but what do I know? I am just a patient; he is the psychiatrist. Dr Metcalfe has his elbows on his desk, his hands forming a steeple.

'The enthusiasm of all the new-age types saying that places like Threeways need to close is not an idea in which I invest much optimism, I am afraid. Inevitably, we will need to care for a core of severe cases. The whole thing will take an age. I will be long gone, you understand.'

Although the words coming from the pasty skin surrounding his lips sound unsure, the subject suddenly seems real. I have so many questions. Anxieties, you might say. You can imagine that, can't you?

At least he didn't say 'you understand' again.

'Where would I have to live?' I ask.

'Oh, you are an eager one, aren't you? I think we might be getting ahead of ourselves there,' says Dr Metcalfe misunderstanding me yet again. He rubs his large, hairy hands together. 'After all, we have to ensure that we are making the right decisions. And for the right reasons. It is all very well listening to a young nurse, but there are a lot of bridges to cross before we get to anything definite.'

I am not sure whether to feel happy or sad at those words. He seems to be saying that there could be a chance of me leaving, but at the same time that it is doubtful. I wonder whether he has his own anxieties? After all, he has been here a long time too. I know you understand what I mean, as even outsiders get anxious about their fate on occasion.

He promises to keep me informed, I suspect via Ron. He tells me that the psychologist was supportive and I would be seeing him for some tests. That sounds scary but it probably is nothing for me to worry about. I know the psychologist, he never wears a tie, it is his way of telling the other staff that he is different, especially the male ones. And he spends most of the time staring at the ceiling and muttering to himself. Like I say, not scary. With that, I realise that Dr Metcalfe is watching me, he grins and nods towards the door for me to leave.

The thing that strikes me most is that this would seem to be confirmation of what I have known for a long time. And what I told you about a while back: that I am not dangerous. I have never even felt dangerous, not like a man I knew on one of the wards who was convinced on a daily basis that he had injured someone. It was not always the same person who was the object of his concerns, merely the standalone anxiety about having harmed another. He lived with that worry every day until he took his own life.

When I get out of Dr Metcalfe' s office, Ron is waiting for me. He looks like he is about to open a Christmas present.

'How did it go?'

'Okay, I suppose.'

'Did he sound keen on my idea?'

'I'm not really sure.' It is the best I can do. The interview passed so swiftly that I need time to think about it. And about Ron's plan. I almost add something about Dr Metcalfe, that he didn't seem to be enthusiastic, but I don't wish to spoil Ron's moment.

'Well, it's a start,' says Ron. He pats me on the back and we part ways. At least he didn't call me a gem. That is Jan's expression. Ron goes to the office, and I go to the day room to light a cigarette. As I do, I notice that my hands are shaking.

## *EXISTENCE*

*We are a speck of dust in the pantheon of life.*
*We are the grey shared bathwater poorly cleansed and*
*unready.*
*We burn the brightest before the fire goes out.*
*The weight of existing has placed impediment to complex*
*relationship.*

*Lunatic, crazy, barmy, nutter, round the twist.*

*The words don't matter. The feeling does.*

# Chapter Twelve

You know I told you that I go to the Box Shop three days a week? Well, on one of the other two mornings, Me, Sid, and Mike go to Occupational Therapy. It is near the chapel, where nobody ever seems to go any more. Do you know that they used to say prayers before every meal? It's true, it was even written in the nursing handbook at one time. 'The Red Book'. They don't call it the Red Book any more. Psychiatry makes a habit of updating these things to make it seem as if improvements are being made, when all they are doing is twiddling the same dial up and down the scale.

Looking forward to things is hard in Threeways, what with the days being the same. But that is not strictly true, because you can look forward to tomorrow when tomorrow is OT. OT is a bit like the Box Shop with less boredom and not so much shouting. The woman that runs the overall area is idiotic. She seems to think that all the women want to knit or cook and all the men want to do woodwork. As it happens, me, Sid and Mike *do* go to the woodwork section. Mike always brings his guitar to woodwork, as if he is waiting to entertain the department. Perhaps one day Mr Jackson will ask him to play a tune or two. Mike is making a magazine rack for the ward. 'It will take pride of place,' that is what Jan the nurse said. Mike's face looked like he had discovered a secret stash of tobacco. I am proud of Mike; he deserves to have his creation on show. Perhaps we will have a special cake to celebrate. He has been working on it for some time now, but you know what they say, all good things come to those who wait.

In the woodwork department at OT, there are loads of tools. Mr Jackson must have been collecting them for years. He has a big board on the wall with all the shapes of the various tools: hammers, rasp files, saws, screwdrivers. That is so we know where to put them. Mr Jackson is an orderly bloke.

Mr Jackson runs the woodwork department, by the way. He has a beard which is patchy. He also has a chubby face and his small ears move when he smiles. He reminds me of a string puppet, operated from above.

He is proud of his tools, is Mr Jackson, so we are always careful to look after them. We would never drop them onto the stone floor here at the woodwork department. Not deliberately, anyway. He has a high KQ, Mr Jackson.

We set to work. Mike is straight on to his magazine rack. I am sanding some table legs, ready for a coat of paint. We rescued them from an office that was being refurbished in the admin block. Funny how they seem to get new stuff over there all the time.

I squint when I am sanding. My eyes are not as sharp as they were. But then, my skin is sagging, my knees ache and my fingers cramp up. Old age comes in a mental hospital as it would anywhere else.

The porter arrives with his metal trolley and gives the post to Mr Jackson.

'Usual rubbish, I suppose?'

The porter agrees and they have a brief chat about the weather. Then the porter taps his trolley and starts off towards the other departments. Mr Jackson flicks through the envelopes, smiling at some, frowning at others. He gets one of his screwdrivers and inserts it into the top of an envelope. As he leaves the room for the coffee room, I hear the ripping sound over his footsteps.

The sawdust on my trousers looks like snow. I brush it off and it falls to the floor—like snow. My attention goes back to the woodwork in front of me. Mike has not seen any of this. He is concentrating on his project.

'How is it coming on, Mike?'

'Oh, pretty good,' he says. He has glue all over his fingers. 'As long as I can get this side stuck on, I should be almost ready for the finishing touches.'

'Just don't glue yourself to the magazine rack, or it won't be much use to the ward.'

Mike laughs. He had originally wanted to make a coat stand, like the one Dr Metcalfe has in his office, but Mr Jackson persuaded him to reconsider. Mike doesn't always know his limitations, as you may have gathered from his guitar playing.

In the middle of the morning, Mr Jackson tells us he is off to see the lady in admin about some paperwork. He wants to order some more tools, apparently. I don't know why; he has loads already. The fact that he leaves us to get on with what we are doing feels good. It is such a nice place to be at woodwork, and because it is set away from the main building, there is no chance of catching a random scream from one of the wards. You can let your mind empty while you are working, and you can have a laugh with your friends. And Mr Jackson, of course. The atmosphere is always relaxed.

We file and scrape and file some more. Mike is engrossed, his tongue is poking out of the corner of his mouth. He starts humming, and then Sid looks up. Sid seems to know the tune, his eyes widen and his whole face lifts when he smiles. He starts to tap his screwdriver on the side of the bench in time to Mike's humming. Mike looks over, his head starts to bob and he smiles back at Sid, who is, by now, singing. The tune bounces back and forth, accelerating between the benches, skimming the floor, rebounding back from the ceiling. There are two other patients here with us, and they are clapping, cheering, encouraging. We all share the performance right until the end. When it's over, there is a celebration like you could not imagine.

When Mr Jackson arrives back, the air is still filled with happiness. As if things couldn't get any better, he has brought back a sponge cake.

'Got this from the cookery group,' he says. He has a proud smile on his face. I told you about his ears, didn't I? They are wiggling. He also has fair hair and ruddy cheeks. I always think he could have been a farmer.

The cake is tasty. Sid declines the offer, claiming that he is dieting, but I know he is joking. He takes the plate and starts to scoff. Mike had already eaten his piece. I wonder for a moment whether we ought to save some for Ray. But then I think the pills have made him large enough already. We wash the cake down with tea.

Thankfully, there is no brandy bottle to top up here. During the break, Mike strums his guitar and the notes, although not particularly connected, they resonate through the department. I think I have said before, there is nothing like real music.

As we start back to work, I realise that I have the pain in my chest again today. I think it is the breakfast. Or it could be the hot air. Or the excitement. Mr Jackson must have noticed me rubbing it because he comes over to me and places his hand on my arm.

'Are you okay, Tim?'

I thump my chest and cough a hacking cough that needs me to take out my handkerchief from my jacket pocket. My brain feels like it is rattling around in my skull, and my throat feels as if someone has attacked it with a cheese grater.

'Chest is a bit sore. Indigestion, I think.'

'Not the cake, I hope. Why don't you sit down? I'll speak to Mrs Drummond. She will organise a cup of tea.'

Did I tell you that Mrs Drummond is the idiot who runs the OT? I don't think I did. She won't like me interrupting the strict routine, but I know the ladies from the knitting room will be only too happy to fuss over me.

'Thank you, Mr Jackson. I think I'll have a ciggie first.'

I go outside and see Mr Jackson's bicycle. Mr Jackson cycles to work every day. His bike looks like it should be rusty, but really it isn't because he takes care to oil the chain and keep the spokes of the wheels clean. Even through his bike has no gears, Mr Jackson cycles up the hill to the OT Department. This is quite a climb because OT is almost at the top of the hospital. Beyond the department are the remains of the farm where Ray works on the gardens. You go past the main gate and up the hill and through the side entrance, which is a gap in the wall with a door. The hill gets pretty steep there so it is a decent climb. I'm guessing Mr Jackson has pretty strong legs for that.

I avoid the puddles on the path and notice the grass is glistening with wet. When I reach the end of the path, I become exposed from the lee of the building. My trousers start to flap in the wind. They are faded, my trousers, and old, like me. But I like them. The sky now looks like it might present some rain in a while. I flip open my lighter and offer the flame to the end of the cigarette. I watch as the white paper ignites and burns orange. I feel the comfort of the refreshing smoke, then I blow it high into the January sky. I feel better for having stood up and got into the fresh air. I think perhaps it was the glue and heat that got into my lungs. Or maybe the sawdust. I notice a robin on a branch and it starts singing. Such a sweet sound. I guess it likes me.

When I look at the hankie, there are the usual green and brown stains, but there is also some red, so I suppose I coughed a bit too hard and strained myself. When I have finished this fag, I think I will go and have that cup of tea with the knitting ladies.

### Elusive Truth

*A sense of the real*
*Is that we know*
*And see how we feel*
*Of elusive truth*
*That nature reveals*

# Chapter Thirteen

What is the point of God? I'm sorry, God, but I mean, I passed the chapel again today and got to thinking. Religions talk about salvation and giving people hope, I realise that, but there does not seem much point in waiting until you are dead for rewards. I am afraid I do not believe in all that. And I do not believe that I am being punished by living most of my life in Threeways, either. I do not believe my present life will be counterbalanced by a hoped-for afterlife. The whole idea of a person watching over us from above in not only sinister, it is ridiculous. I have been watched over for years by real people who judge me, so why do I need God to do it as well?

Sorry about that, but today I am feeling down. There are times of reflection, despite the monotony of it all. In my early days at the hospital, the times when my brain was not in forced lethargy because of the pills, I would think about having another life. I would talk as I walked, conversing with anyone who wanted to listen, even if there was no one to listen. Words rattled about in my head like stones in a cement mixer. Some of the thoughts had to be surrendered as unhelpful, killed off like a sack of unwanted cats. There are times when a mental patient finds it hard to distinguish which thoughts are useful, let me tell you, but I never mentioned murdering these thoughts, as that would have attracted the wrong attention and more experimental drugs.

Earlier on I heard the staff chatting at handover. It is not nice to eavesdrop, but I heard my name mentioned.

'Tim should be ideal.' This was Ron talking. 'I've done the referral to the rehab team. I've also lined up a visit.'

Visit? Either someone is coming to see me or Ron is expecting me to go somewhere.

'Oh, he's a gem, our Tim. I would seem strange without him.' No need to see her face. That was Jan.

They spoke about some more stuff that I did not follow entirely. Something about hospital policy information. Then I had to stop listening for a moment because a porter arrived onto the ward with some post. By the time I got back within earshot, they had started talking about the fact that they were all going out tonight. They go out every month, or as near as they can get to it. I wonder where they go and what they talk about. I suppose they talk about us, our strange habits and our aggressive ways. But we keep them in a job, that is one way of looking at it.

Ron was talking about his project again yesterday. I sort of agreed because I don't want to upset him. It's my own fault, really, I asked him some questions because I had been thinking about it in woodwork, as I was sanding the table leg. Funny what you think about, isn't it? I didn't mean to give him the wrong impression, but I think maybe I did. I do hope I don't let him down.

After meeting Dr Metcalfe, and hearing Ron's enthusiasm, I am starting to believe that moving could be real. What I do not know is if I get a choice. I decide to put it out of my mind and wait and see what it is all about when he mentions it again. I really don't think I want to be doing laundry and cooking every day though. When he first mentioned it, the idea of leaving whirred in my brain all night. When I thought about not being here anymore, it struck me that Threeways provides my feeling of belonging. It is part of me, it runs through me as much as our madness is woven into the stonework of Threeways. My only qualification in life is to have survived here. You might say I simply surrendered, but it takes more than that to keep going, let me tell you. And then there is Millie, I would miss her. Millie has no limit in her capacity for goodness. It is like she refills every time she hands out love, or kindness. Her KQ is like a kettle left on the stove. Boiling over.

I will talk to Ron and tell him my concerns. I need to talk to him about Williams as well. Perhaps I will do both things at once.

Do you remember Ralf? He is the one who thought he was Henry VIII. I heard today that he wrote a letter to Princess Anne. It wasn't very legible, apparently, but sufficiently so that they knew the address. In the letter, Ralf said that he was a secret agent, and he knew of a Russian plot to blow up Buckingham Palace. They returned the letter to the ward and Ralf was told off. He has a thing about the royals. There was another man I remember who claimed that he was the Russian Tsar, Nicholas II. He used to talk about his Imperial Army and how he would regain control of his Motherland. He insisted on wearing a makeshift sash, which he made out of an old pillow case. The nurses were told not to encourage him, and they always changed the subject. The doctors tried to convince him about reality. They are concerned with reality in Threeways. The staff, that is. What they fail to understand is that reality inside the walls is different from that the other side. I figure Nicholas was entitled to think that's who he was if he wanted. He's dead now, anyway, so it doesn't matter anymore.

The staff are all out getting drunk, and I feel happy back on the ward. Life is quieter in the evenings. That is because of the night-time tranquillisers they dish out. Earlier, me and Mike played Monopoly, but it was inconclusive and we got fed up. We wondered whether we should play cards after that, but we didn't. It is ten o'clock now and most people have either gone to bed or are having an evening drink. My friend Mike and me, we are now smoking and watching the telly. There is nobody talking about radio transmitters or chosen frequencies or moon landings or secret bank accounts. We have a lot of that here. I am lucky like that. I have never had voices, not real nasty ones. The only one I have is the normal one that talks in your head and I assume that everyone has that.

Mike is younger than me. I do not know how he came to be in Threeways and we have never really spoken about it at length. I do know that he lived with his mum and dad above their newsagent shop in the town. His dad used to get up before dawn to sort the newspapers, so when Mike was old enough he started doing the same and helping out. Then he started doing the deliveries on his bicycle. As far as I can see, he was a faithful son and a polite advocate for the shop. His dad would let him have some sweets from behind the counter as payment for helping out. One day, and this is about as much as I know, Mike began to feel strange. He said he started putting the newspapers in a bin near his school. It did not take long before the customers were complaining. The events must have overtaken him, as they do for some people. His direction towards the innerworld of our existence was set.

Mike's mum has visited him here. She has not been for a long time and I wonder if she has passed away. She used to bring him sweets when she came, which reminded him of his past. Mike might have asked her to stop coming.

Me and Mike laugh together at the flickering images on the telly. As we do, I look at the flooring, yellowed with years of mopping and floor polish. On mornings when I do not have to go out, I watch the domestics swirl their machines about on the floor. Now the ash from Mike's cigar has fallen onto it, and lies there, a fat grey cylinder. He usually flicks it into the plant pot at the side of the chair where he normally sits, but I guess he miscalculated.

Linda is a Scottish lady. She has a coffee mug in her hand as she comes into the day room.

'Can we switch the telly over? *The Sweeney* is on.'

Her voice is squeaky.

'Yes, of course. We're not really watching it anyway,' I tell her.

'I like *The Sweeney*,' says Mike.

'Didn't have you down as a Sweeney fan, Linda,' I say.

'Oh, well. My father was a policeman in Aberdeen. I don't think he was as rough as these cops on the telly, but I suppose that's what gave me an interest.'

'Ha ha.' I hear laughter coming from an adjacent chair. It is Ray laughing at the Radio Times.

'Morecambe and Wise. On Saturday night. Bloody marvellous.'

I feel like telling Ray he has missed it, because it is Sunday, but I opt against it. Let him enjoy his laughter. Me and Mike decide to get a coffee and some of the leftover cake from our visit to OT and leave Linda to enjoy her programme.

Television: the gateway to other worlds. The flickering pictures tell me about other places, almost as much as the books I read in the library. The images show me what happens outside Threeways and I think I have said before that it is not all good. After a while, you almost forget about the otherworld, you become so plugged in to life here that things outside are unreal.

My mind turns to the ward staff, they will be talking about largactil and sharing stories about Threeways, they love to do that. I remember hearing one of their favourite stories with all the Bible stuff about Cliff, who they call a 'large schizophrenic'. He was on Ward 14. For some staff, Cliff was regarded as intimidating, and he was religious and psychotic, always a fun mix. I can hear them now: 'Oh yes. I remember a time when Father Donaly visited him and Cliff locked the two of them in a side room together. He said that he was protecting them from the evils of Satan.' 'Father?' says the head nurse, 'he was just a local vicar who dropped into the wards to spread Christian dogma. Serves him right what happened, you get too close to them and too chummy and they take advantage. My dad would soon have dealt with a maverick patient like that.' He nods to himself and flicks his cigarette ash. 'I remember that story,' says another nurse. 'He kept him in there for an hour and a half. There was no way he was letting him out. The sound of Cliff singing 'Onward Christian Soldiers' coming from the other side of the door kept us all amused. At one stage, the whole ward seemed to be talking to him through the door. It was only the fact that teatime arrived that Cliff relented.' Head nurse replies, 'Oh yeah, he was fond of his food, old Cliff.'

They will go on in their drunken way, wondering whether Father Donaly ever came back to the ward after that. I suppose what I am saying when I talk about a story like that, is that Father – or whatever he was – Donaly, he was not able to influence the patient, so he gave up. I think perhaps that Ron will eventually feel the same when he realises that his idea is not for me.

I will leave the staff to their alcoholic enjoyment and make my way to the dorm. Any anxieties I have about moving will be buried in the depths of sleep.

### *Untitled*

*Stolen thoughts sink in the West*
*Dragged away by the setting sun*

*Forests of hope*
*Full of trees where Dreams hang*

*Spirits stalk the ground*

*Sea and Stars and Skies and*
*Voices and the Serpent of noise*

*Feeds on the cries of the*
*People inside*

*Spurned and despised*

# Chapter Fourteen

The poetry? Ah, well, since you ask, I have been writing it for some years. I cannot tell you how long, because time is like an accordion, it ebbs and flows. There have been times when some of the pills they gave me actually. Would you believe that? They made me hallucinate and I would write the images in my poetry. Or maybe I was hallucinating anyway. It was hard to tell at times. I read poetry too. And I'm in good company, because Ezra Pound was in a mental hospital.

I get inspiration by my favourite book, the one by my friend Philip.

I write stories as well. Nobody else knows about them. I don't need to share them, because they are personal, mostly. But I am making an exception for you. Certain things inspire me: the weather, flowers, other patients, Millie. When you are a writer, you cannot help but notice the things around you.

### Echoes

*The echo of being falls into the void;*
*Meaning and purpose are blurred*
*Fickle fate hovered at my table*
*Then flew away like a small bird*

# Chapter Fifteen

Music is some classical stuff. Me and Sid and Mike have made the effort, as usual. The rest look like they have come to fall asleep. In a way that is a shame because music offers an escape, in a way that a good book can take you into another place. Music does the same thing but quicker and easier. I guess that is what Ron would like to hear. I should tell him that one day.

Edward has on a chequered bow tie and he is reading a book. His glasses are halfway down his nose and he hardly notices us arrive. Edward is like me, he has been here for ages and wants to live life untroubled. It is like we have been in the waiting room at Charing Cross watching the people pass by. I understand the French call their waiting rooms 'the room of lost steps.' I like that.

The Blue Room is warm, which is good because it is really cold outside. I saw Ron peering out of the window earlier. He was muttering about the snow, about it dragging the branches of the trees. It was quite a nice image. I have stored it and will use it in my poems. We are both artists and tinkers. A pulsating mass of humanity inaccessible to the experts who fiddle and pick and nibble at the edges.

The thought is countered by Marjorie. I think she functions in spite of herself. Her anger rises in relation to a lack of cigarettes as much as anything. She is like distant rolling thunder sent down from Nordic gods.

Her temper gets signalled long before she appears. Today, she has managed to find her way over from her ward on time. She has been sitting slouched in a chair at the end of the day room, yelling incoherent rants. A discerning passer-by might be able to pick up the occasional obscenity.

When she starts shuffling towards the group, Ron heads her off. He plies her with some cash and three cigarettes. Marjorie grins, her bearded chin scrunching into a gurn because of her lack of teeth. Ron is a clever bugger sometimes, he knows she would simply disrupt the music. He looks pleased with himself as he announces the programme.

'You should find the music this week very stirring,' says Ron. 'These Russian composers used energy and vitality in their music.'

It sounds like he has been reading up again.

'Does that mean there be any Rimsky-Korsakov today then, Ron?' asks Edward. Of course he is here. I told you he likes opera and classical music.

Ron starts checking the album cover.

'Yes, Scheherazade.'

Edward nods as if to affirm his approval. 'Lovely.'

'Russian composers,' says Sid in a soft tone. 'Was Chekhov a Russian composer, Ron?'

This seems to arouse Mike's interest. 'Chekhov is in *Star Trek*, isn't he, Ron?'

'You're right, Mike, there is a character in *Star Trek* called Chekhov, but I don't think that is who Sid is referring to.'

'I love *Star Trek*,' says Neil. 'Captain Kirk and Spock.'

'Not *Star Trek*!' Ron insists.

Now Ray joins the discussion. 'I like the Klingons.'

'And the Daleks,' says Neil.

'Yeah. Bloody well exterminate everyone.' Sid is suddenly back in default mode. I worry about Sid. He gets down. More so than I do. I see

'That's *Doctor Who*, Neil.'

'*Doctor Who*. Ha ha.'

Ron looks like he wishes his group was called, 'Popular TV Shows'.

'No, no, no.' Ron intervenes. 'Look, this is about Russian composers, people who write music. It's not about television.'

'Actually, Sid, Chekhov was a playwright,' says Edward. 'But he was Russian, so you were partly right. Not a composer though.'

I have asked the question before. What does he expect? This time, I am not sure he expects too much, though. He was out with the staff last night. I expect he took Claire. Claire is his girlfriend, and if you want to know something funny, she works in the ECT clinic. Why is that funny? Well, I told you before how much Ron hates ECT, and yet he sees Claire. I don't blame him for that, though. She is really pretty, with long blonde hair and sparkly blue eyes. She also has freckles on her nose. I remember her when she was a student nurse. She smiled at me every time I saw her. I think she smiles at every person she sees. No wonder Ron likes her too. Sometimes, she comes to the ward to see him and we catch up. Last time, she told me all about her new scooter that she uses to get to work. It is yellow, she has told me that. It isn't quite the sports car that the young doctors drive and park over outside the admin block, but she likes it.

The lady who runs ECT is called Bridget. She is another one of those sour-faced types like Sister Saunders, but there is less chance of Sister Bridget smiling than her. I don't know why we call Sister Saunders by her surname and Sister Bridget by her forename. I never considered that before.

Claire reminds me of that Millais painting of Ophelia. She is a lovely girl (high KQ) and I don't know how she endures working with the Bridget. I expect she switches off, you know, detaches herself like I described earlier. I am no expert but it seems to me that the ability to defocus is a useful one in many aspects of life. I do it at IT, it helps the morning go by, so why shouldn't the nurses do the same? It is just that, in their case, it seems wrong, what with them dealing with people. I don't blame Claire, though, if that is what she does. In her case, she would do it to block Sister Bridget. I can't imagine Claire ignoring the patients she cares for; she is too sweet for that. Her type of nurse has a kindness founded on the oldest principles of human goodness.

The Russian music is stirring, as Ron promised. Edward is pleased.

'Lovely to hear Mussorgsky, Ron,' he says.

139

Nobody else knows what he is talking about. I'm not sure Ron would if he did not have the album cover on his lap. Anyway, Ron nods and looks satisfied. After the group I am going to get Philip out of my locker and read through a couple of my favourite poems. *Long Lion Days*, I think. And then *The Old Fools*.

The afternoon passes, as it always does, with cigarettes, patient watching, chatting to the nursing staff. Now it is suppertime. I can already hear the clanking of the food trolley as the porter unloads the food from his wagon. A rich aroma passes through the ward and actually smells half decent.

After collecting our food, me and Mike sit with Ray. The food is almost as good as it smelt. The shepherd's pie is meaty with rich gravy and the carrots look crunchy.

Ray is sitting in his usual chair, his large body filling most of his side of the table. He is a robust man, and if I think Mr Jackson could have been a farmer, Ray almost certainly was. Ray is fond for eating. In fact, whenever he sits down to a meal, he stares at the plate in wonder. His eyes widen and his ruddy face beams. A pirate standing by a treasure chest on which he has just lifted the lid could not look more excited. He claps his massive hands together.

'Fabulous! I like shepherd's pie. Five carrots, potato, gravy, fabulous!'

We start to eat, Mike and me. Just across from us on an adjacent table are two other patients, Clive and Martin.

'I hate it here,' says Clive. He is bent over his plate so that his face is almost in his supper. 'I want to move.'

Although the comment seems more like he is thinking out loud, Martin picks up the topic.

'I run this place. I own this hospital.'

'Bloody hate it,' repeats Clive under his breath.

The two of them start an interchange of monologues and start a one-man conversation together.

'I have millions and billions of pounds. Trillions probably.'

'We'll all go to Hell,' says Clive.

'I'm going to have the managers all fired. And I'm going to order that the nurses are given a pay rise. Woolies gave me a radio you know.'

'Stuck in Hell.' Clive's imagery is descending

'I might have this place shut down by the authorities. I know the Prime Minister.'

Up to this point, they don't seem aware of the other's conversation, but this comment makes Clive look up.

'I wish you would.' His tone is sincere enough.

The two of them scrape their plates and Martin gets up and leaves to have a smoke.

Clive's thoughts are still being let loose like a flickering ember.

'Hate it.'

'He's got a point, though,' Mike says, speaking between mouthfuls of food, most of which seems to be on his chin.

'Who has?'

Mike peers at me and nods his head over to the other table. 'Clive. He hates it here. Didn't you hear him?'

The day is ending as it started: without much fuss. I am watching the telly, specifically, the Open University programmes. It is probably time to turn in. I don't care for the look of Module H23, *Quantum Mechanics for the Real World*. I also don't care for the sickly sweet lavender and candy smell of the deodorant the nurse is wearing. Some of the night staff like to chat, unlike the day staff, they come out of their office and sit in the day room. They have coffee and a smoke with me. My favourite nurse is Keres, she comes from Greece. I would have preferred her to be called Aphrodite or Athena, but there you are. Keres tells me about the blue sky and the deserted beaches and the Aegean Sea. I asked her if she was from Athens because it was the only place I know in Greece. She is from Thessaloniki, a place to the east by the sea. She says that as a child she used to visit her grandfather in Crete. She told me all about the myth of the Minotaur and the stories her grandfather told her about the island. She also told me about the food, with lots of lamb dishes. It is a strange thing, but whenever I think of her I think about those blue skies and Greek gods and tankers. Tankers as in oil tankers, because I looked up Greece in a book in the library and it had a story about Aristotle Onassis. From his picture he looks distinguished and a typical looking Greek person. He has huge wealth; he is one of the richest people in the world. I expect he has more money than Martin, who you remember has millions and billions of pounds.

Keres is not here tonight, only the nurse with the lavender deodorant, so I finish my cigarette, say goodnight and go to the dormitory.

When I reach my bed, I lie on the top of the covers and contemplate the fragmented chat I overheard while eating tea. Why was it that this particular conversation caught my attention? And why now? Clive may be irrational but his message was clear. He hates it here. Clive's vision of Threeways as Hell suggests a kaleidoscopic image. When I consider the daily routines at Threeways, it isn't that bad. Like today when I helped out on the geriatric ward. I have friends here and I don't want for much, I am safe. I have never really thought any more than a day at a time. Things just happen.

I lie awake for a while, listening to the noises of the night. I make a mental note to write a poem about that.

I realise that in all of the time I have been in the hospital, I have never had great cause to worry about my life. It all gets blocked off, like life falling into a sponge or a bag of flour. Most of all I never used to worry about the future. Hearing Clive makes me think though, and now I understand that I am a world away from the things I see on the television. I know what I am and I know my life is in here, in the innerworld. If I were a younger man, a fitter man, I might consider leaving. It is the familiar and not hopelessness that makes me stay. Not like the old men on the chronic wards where they stick those poor buggers who have lost their sense of self. They couldn't care less what day of the week it is, or whether their clothes are clean. They shuffle about in a cloud of bewilderment. Maybe that is a nice thing. Ignorance is bliss, they say. Only I do not think that counts in Threeways.

## BRAIN

*The crack'd brains that bash against one another, the alpha waves from inner caves, the brain music of the madman that others fail to comprehend.*

# Chapter Sixteen

Tuesdays should be just another day. All the days are pretty similar here. Friday is woodwork, and it is always nice to finish the week with woodwork. But today is Tuesday, and Tuesday is a Box Shop day. That's never one to look forward to.

We pass from the cold outside and into the gloom. We hang our coats in the usual place. Then we go to our benches and start work. They call it work. It is not something I want to argue about. I like to try and defocus, like I have already said. There are times, though, when I wonder what I might have done for work. If I wasn't in Threeways, that is. I was strong when I was younger, and I'm tall. I could have been a postman, or a baker. No, not a baker, they have to get up really early every day to bake the bread. That wouldn't have appealed to me. I'm not really all that good in the early mornings. Perhaps a butcher, then? Yes, a butcher, I can see me heaving the carcasses about, slapping them on the slab for cutting. I think I might have made a fine butcher.

The coughing chorus starts soon after I get to the bench. I'm as guilty as any, but I do my best to suppress the urges, because I know Williams hates the noise. Rattling chests and constricted airways are part of the soundtrack here. I remember going to the General for a chest x-ray once. I have no idea what it showed. A surrealist image of blackened broccoli, I suppose. I hear Sid sigh beside me, obviously waiting for the tortuous process to begin. Another day in the heavenly surroundings of the Box Shop. I worry about Sid. He gets down. More so than I do. I seem to be able to think my way out of the gloom. Sid has no volition. Life has beaten it out of him. I worry that one day it will get too much and he will take the final trip too early.

I prepare my packages, forming them into a row. Then I stack the finished boxes into a pile, like the wall of a house. You have to have a system. It helps to numb the brain to the stupidity of the process. Everyone has a different method: some people chose to put their cardboard on the left and drag across to the right, some do it the other way. Others have a random approach, cardboard scattered in front of them, not caring where they get the next template from.

The department is cold. I can see the breath of the patient opposite me. He has his hair shaved above his ears, and a golden spray of what remains sprouts from the top of his head. He counts mechanically to himself as he folds the walls of the boxes. I watch for a moment: one, two, three, four…There! He grins and emits a short chuckle which is contained in his throat. His pride, which mingles with apparent astonishment at his achievement, is evident.

It doesn't take long for Williams to appear, prowling around the desks, inspecting the workers, trying to find an excuse to start on someone. He walks with his hands behind his back, his pencil is lodged behind his ear. He has a cigarette between his thin blue lips.

There have been times I have wondered whether I ought to feel some sympathy for Williams. I know that sounds stupid, but any person who treats others the way he does must be unhappy themselves. I consider if he might have been treated badly himself, or if he hates his job. It may be that perhaps he hates people. I do not see how you can hate people for the sake of it, though, that makes no sense. Surely you have to have a reason to behave that way? The problem is, no matter how you try, I do not see how you justify cruelty. If he was ever capable of kindness, it seems that it would take a miracle for the virtue to come back out.

Just as I am having these thoughts I see Williams creeping about. His progress is deliberately slow, like a game of musical chairs with a sadistic twist. When will the music stop? I feel sure it will be Sid, but I am wrong.

'Useless foreigner,' he hisses to an unprotected ear. 'Foreign shit.'

It might have been the lad opposite with the blond hair and the protruding tongue. It might have been anybody. But today it is Jakub. Jakub is Polish. Luckily for Williams, Jakub doesn't understand too well. He is one of the remnants from the war; a casualty, you might say. There were a lot of them here at first, mostly pilots, like Jakub, but their numbers have dwindled

148

from illness and the ravages of depression. He is the only one who is still able to work at the Box Shop because the others are either too old or infirm. War wounds are lasting. Lost arms make working in the Box Shop an impossibility.

Jakub opts for silence. He has given up hope on life, I can sense it when I see him. Someone once said that he had been in a concentration camp at the end of the war. I don't know if that is true, but if it is, he would have faced worse than Williams in his time.

'Fucking hopeless,' says Williams. 'Just like the rest of your useless race.'

Should I intervene? My chest is filling with poison and starting to hurt even more. I resent the implication that Jakub and his people didn't stand up to Hitler. It is unfair. They were men who battled hard and often paid a high price. The highest price in some cases. I wonder to myself what Williams did back then. He's the type who hides away, or pretends to have something wrong with him so that he doesn't have to fight.

'You can't even understand me, chum, can you?'

I decide that Williams is lucky to have the stoicism of Jakub. A man who has seen stinking piles of rotting bodies and dismembered limbs won't be affected by a bit of shouting. Part of me wants him to react, though. What a surprise Williams would have if he were rounded on by a battle-hardened soldier. Sadly, although I think Williams is taking a risk, he knows that Jakub is not going to be provoked. And I am not going to make things any worse for him or me by butting in. In some respects, it makes it better that Williams is simply frustrated by the interaction.

Suddenly, as Williams is about to relaunch his campaign of hatred, Jakub turns his head and stares directly at him. Whether it is the pace with which he moves, which is sinister enough, or the steel in the dark eyes, I am not certain, but I watch as Williams takes a half step back. What a satisfying sight. The bully confronted. His face is fixed with fear. Williams waves an agitated hand and retreats, his boots backtracking all the way to his office. When the door slams, I think I hear a chuckle from the opposite bench.

Good old Jakub, taking the sting out of Williams so that my friend Sid gets a day off. Heart warming. Or, in my case, chest warming.

Now, let's get to building my cardboard stack.

# Chapter Seventeen

We have finished breakfast, and I am sitting in the day room, reclining in a chair. I am having a cigarette, listening to Mike practice his guitar. I take a drag and stare up at the ceiling.

'What are you learning now, Mike?'

'Er, um…Some Beatles. *Yellow Submarine*, actually.'

'That's good. Is it getting easier?'

'A bit. I'm thinking of getting an electric guitar soon.'

I shiver at the thought of Mike's amplified efforts reverberating around the room. I can't imagine that they will allow his sound to fill the vast spaces on the ward. I can see all manner of complications, not least of which is the likelihood of upsetting other patients. I can see Mike's guitar being smashed over his head. They will shoo him off to *Fags and Shags*, I suspect.

'What are you planning to do today?'

Mike broke off from his practice and thought about the question.

'Nothing much. A bit of practicing after the Box Shop.'

'Music?' He looks at me. 'Group, I mean.'

'I suppose,' he says, now looking down at his fingers, trying to contort them into a chord shape.

Neil barges past, not saying anything. He looks grumpy, so I follow him to investigate.

I find him in the Blue Room, that being the quietest place on the ward. He is surrounded by his smoking debris, which is laid out untidily on the table before him. Martin is in here with him and he is sitting with his elbows resting on his knees and his hands clasped to his temples. He sounds unhappy.

'I'm having a heart attack.'

Silence.

'My dad left me this place in his will.'

Neil ignores him. He is pushing bits of tobacco around the table as if organising his stash. Martin continues, unconcerned by the lack of response.

'I ought to shut the place down. I'm not well, I have a stinking cold...' He strikes a match, lights a cigarette and pulls the coffee table ashtray towards him. Then he looks up at me momentarily. 'The nurses are getting a pay rise. I'll take the money from my petrol company in Saudi Arabia.'

Still Neil is disinterested. He is now busy shuffling what remains of his tobacco on the table in front of him. He has cigarette papers that are smudged with the ash from his fingers, and three or four matches. He occasionally retrieves a lighter from his jacket pocket and attempts to spark it. But every time he does, he finds they are dead.

This pattern continues, with Martin rambling his thoughts and Neil maintaining a manful silence. There is nothing I can do here.

# THOUGHTS

*Fleeting, disconnected, associated with discordant rhythm, pauses are over-played, frozen in time, suspended by the unwelcome interlopers or delayed by decaying dendrites, eventually squeezed like a fetid turd or an oversized baby into the world, proudly presented, maintained and reinforced.*

I just wrote that. The humdrum feel on the ward made me feel at a loose end. Mike was lost in the attempted chord sequence of his latest song. When I finished writing the poem, I decided to go out walking in the grounds.

'Going anywhere nice?' Jan saw me putting on my coat.

'Not sure.'

'Done your bed?'

'Yes, bed's made.'

'Well done, Tim. You're a real gem.'

'See what I mean? No bother, me.'

I considered going to the library, but I don't fancy reading today. Did I say that I am normally the only one in there? Apart from the librarian, that is. Not many patients use it, actually. Edward goes there, but he mostly reads novels.

Outside, I see the head nurse heading home in his beaten up old car. He crunches the gears and I can see him lighting a cigarette. As I watch the car go down the drive, he winds the window down and tips the contents of his car ashtray onto the verge. A few more butts will make no difference.

As I wander, I think about Ron's plan again. I think about the people and things I will leave behind. I also think about whether I should pay more attention to my sore chest. It seems to trouble me more when the subject of Ron's project comes up.

Then I start thinking about being outside Threeways. Then I think of all the years I have been in Threeways. There is not much to encourage you to think about your past. Best left in darkened rooms, smudged onto the walls like ancient cave drawings.

I see there are some smart-looking men in suits and wonder if they are here for a tribunal.

Nothing remarkable ever happens here. We never get spectacular events like a fire, even though the fire brigade seem to be called out by false alarms all the time. I remember a small fire in the kitchens once, but it did not amount to much. There was a flood on the ward not long ago, someone climbed onto a basin to open a window, I do not know why. It might have been to let smoke out, or to get a view of the clock tower, it does not matter, really. All I know is that the basin collapsed, and the patient wrenched a pipe of the wall that he was using for leverage. One of the nurses came running into the day room shouting. 'Water everywhere…pipes burst. Better call maintenance.'

Ron came out of the office to investigate. When he saw the extent of the problem, he almost shrieked. 'Oh hell,' he said. 'Somebody tell me that Noah is on the way!' I probably should not have done, but I laughed. I could not help it.

Neil was hovering around, watching the hullabaloo and stomping first one leg and then the other in a crazy funny dance of delight.

'Get the bloody mop out, Ron. Ha ha ha!'

'Yes, Neil,' said Ron, 'good idea, get the bloody mop out.'

Neil wasn't about to do anything. He continued his hysterical laughter, His entire body first lurched backwards and then doubled up as his nose almost hit his knee. He stamped his foot back down into the floor and it made a splashing noise, spraying water over the walls. The staff ran around in a panic as the cold water continued to gush out of the severed pipework. This just made Neil laugh even more. Ron had sent the student nurse and the auxiliary off the to the laundry cupboard for towels. The water was everywhere. At the same time, he tried to stem the other flow, that of the patients. The last thing he needed was someone slipping over and having to deal with a medical problem as well. By this time, there was a gathering crowd.

'Oh dear me.' Linda's little Scottish voice understated the concern.

'You need to call maintenance,' said Mike, who had his guitar over his back.

By this time, Ron had removed his shoes and socks. He was on his hands and knees placing towels onto what was fast becoming a small lake. He looked up. 'Thanks, Mike.'

In the midst of the panic, Ray sloshed through the water in the hallway, a bough wave ahead of every footstep. He walked past Ron and his flood defence team.

'Off to the gardens. Be back for lunch. Lovely day out today.' He rubbed his hands together. 'Fabulous.'

Ron shook his head in disbelief as he watched him leave.

The maintenance engineers arrived to reprimand Ron for not having turned the water off at the isolator. The water had managed to soak through to the day room. It reached halfway to Dr Metcalfe's office.

Ron asked, 'How was I supposed to know?'

'You've been here long enough,' said the maintenance man.

Luckily for Ron, Metcalfe was on holiday, and by the time he got back all evidence of the problem was gone.

Anyway, I got sidetracked. I was talking about these men in the suits and the tribunal. You see these once in a while when a patient wants to appeal against a section. It strikes me as strange because it is safe here. As far as I can see, there is plenty to worry about on the other side of the hospital wall. I mean, I see things on TV: wars and bombing and fighting, kidnapping, hijacking, murders. The real world looks like a scary place.

When I look at everything about me here, there is so much natural beauty, it was a shame to create such chaos. One thing we never had here was a lake. It might have been nice to see a lake with a crust of ice in the winter, and a dense mist hanging over the surface in the spring. In summer, we would have had water lilies that would have reminded me of my favourite Monet painting in the art book. I know why we do not have a lake though, because a lake would be too tempting for people to throw themselves in and end up like Virginia Woolf. We do not want to place temptation in the way of the loonies, oh no.

I pass the Superintendent's House. It is a marvel, a splendour. But does he really need a grand driveway sweeping up to the main door and elaborate stone carvings *and* a sunken Italian Garden at the front? Around the back there is an ornamental pond and a conservatory and two tennis courts. *Two.* Beyond that is a wooded area. How fancy for someone running an asylum. The superintendent is the head of the hospital, by the way. The head psychiatrist, if you like. He is the one that all the other doctors worry about. Like I worry about Williams, or Dr Metcalfe. There is a serious ranking order in Threeways.

The cricket pitch slopes away from the back garden of the house. As I walk around the outside, hidden amongst the weeds and long grass, I notice an old roller. It is a huge rusted iron contraption. They used to use it to hand roll the middle of the pitch before the season started. Now look at it: forlorn, unused, forgotten. There is a machinery graveyard in the grounds, where they dump all the outdated and broken equipment: the chairs, catering tables, laundry equipment. They are all there, behind a high fence. All forgotten. That is what I will be one day. One day, I will be gone from here, and not how Ron thinks. I will leave in a box, which is ironic considering what we do at IT. The hospital will go the same way eventually. The trees will still be here, but the bushes will be overgrown, the grass will be long and the weeds will overwhelm the gardens. Visitors will see broken windows, and on what is now the place where the junior doctors park their sports cars, there will be piles of rubble: metal bed frames, rotten floorboards and old doors. It will be hard to make out the signs, indicating their former use as a toilet or a psychiatrist's office, and time will have stripped them of any significance. They will be equalised so that rank no longer has meaning. The pavilion that now stands so proud and white in front of me will be nothing more than a bird sanctuary, with only the distant echoes of shouting and frolicking patients.

Best of all, when I think of it, is the dreaded Industrial Therapy block. I see the window sills are now no more than a place where weeds can grow. The tiles are slipping off the sagging roof. The department sits in dilapidated misery; an aged boxer, reduced to his knees by the passage of time. Williams is nothing but a distant memory, overtaken by the clocks and fed to the worms.

What a joyous thought and an unexpected pleasure.

I am still feeling buoyant when I near *Fags and Shags* and hear the piano. This is part of our neglected abilities, part of our wonderful existence that is denied when we are caught in the blinding light of judgement. Nobody has played that for as long as I can remember. It just sits there, at the end of the room. I open the door and go in, to find lots of patients. Most of them are smiling. Now I see why Ron thinks his group was a good idea. I realise that he has the wrong focus. It is *real* music that people like. I decide to make a suggestion for one of the groups so that we all get the chance to play a musical instrument, whether we can or, in Mike's case, not. Sorry, Mike, that was mean.

I see Mad Geoff doing his mad dance. That also sounds mean, calling him Mad Geoff, but everyone calls him that. His long ginger hair bounces like copper snakes as his legs move about, whirling him around. He is bobbing and jumping, his arms rotating like the propeller of a rudderless ship. He is happy though, as usual. Nobody can understand Geoff because he mumbles and laughs all the time, but I don't often see him miserable.

As I get my tea, the lady behind the counter smiles. I have seen her here before. She is a large lady who dresses in flowing dresses, waistcoats over her blouse and leather sandals. She wears her brown hair loose and parted in the centre, sometimes with headband. She is new. Her badge says 'Tina'.

'Nice, isn't it?'

I smile back, feeling like the day is improving. 'Yes,' I say. 'It is lovely, Tina.'

### *Sound*

*A note of sound*
*In a glowing mist*
*A futile grasp*
*From a fragile fist*

# Chapter Eighteen

'Morning, Tim.' I hear a familiar voice and peel open my eyes, parting the crust to see Neil standing over my bed.

'What's up, Neil?'

Although he is smiling, he appears nervous. His fingers are in and out of his trouser pockets. He gets like this at times.

'Can you take me to the social later, for a cup of tea?'

'Are you okay, Neil?' I notice that he is already fully dressed, in his grey/white shirt and his light-blue, gravy-stained tie. His tweed jacket is missing a button.

Neil ignores my question. 'Can we go the social, Tim?'

'Of course, Neil, I have to go to Ward Eighteen this morning, but I could see you when I get back. I will come and find you later.'

It seems to do the trick because he lopes off. His stooping gait; like a giraffe with a hangover, is recognisable to anyone.

I stretch and scratch my head. It's cold in the dorm. I don't fancy getting up, but the morning is awakening around me like a stirring bear. In the dorm, I smell the rotting shoes, stale farts, nicotine and halitosis. I decide to move before the male staff appear and start tipping up beds.

I have not always been on Ward 1. I have been on several wards at Threeways. I was in a secure ward once upon a time. On that ward, we were woken by the clanking of keys in locks. They still have keys in Threeways. Keys are important here. They signify power to some. All the wards have a bunch of keys for various doors and cupboards. They are guarded by the person in charge, and they are so important that some nurses wear them like a badge. For others, they are like an item of jewellery. The mental nurses joke about the 'real' nurses at the General. They laugh at how they spend their days scurrying from one area to another with their fob watches bouncing off their chests. The way I see it, the keys are as much a symbol as the watch, only the staff at Threeways prefer to drink coffee and sit in the office.

In the bathroom, I run the water for a shave. My razor is so blunt, I am surprised that I still have skin on my face. When I look in the mirror, I see the grey spreading, taking over my dark hair like an invading army. I realise that the years are advancing. A new front is being breached every day as my time runs out, the ebbing of life, the running out of the sand, the retreat of my existence. All of this makes me think I have been spending too long with Sid. This is not a subject that normally concerns me, and perhaps it is the thought of Ron talking of trying to move me. I shake my head and run my shaving brush around the soap.

After breakfast, when the three of us are ready, I go into the staff office to tell the head nurse that we are leaving. He is sitting back in his chair reading the paper, as usual. He bends the corner down and nods a grunting noise in my direction. I know what he is thinking: just another day

Our work party sets off down the corridor towards Ward Eighteen. You can pass any number of people in the corridors. We share them with the porters and the bustling nurses. And the loping social workers in their suede shoes. And the click-clacking psychiatrists. This morning, the light is reflecting off the blue and white ceramic on the walls giving a snow globe effect to the dust particles.

Ward Eighteen is a female geriatric ward. I ring the bell and wait. They have to keep the door locked here because they don't want the old ladies wandering off and breaking a hip. Or pissing and shitting all over the corridors.

Most of the ladies have simply grown old in the hospital, usually getting confused in the process. For the second time today, I will be welcomed by a pungent aroma. This time it is the ammonia of urine and cleaning fluid that assaults the nostrils. One of the nurses lets me in and sure enough, the smell is breathtaking. Literally, it takes your breath away. I am met by Jean. Jean is one of the patients, a slightly built lady with short white hair and an engaging nature. Due to her worsening memory and confusion, she always seems to be worried and agitated about something or other. Funny how she always greets me like a long lost relative.

'Hello, my love. How are you?'

I knew she doesn't know me, but it can't hurt to be pleasant, I always think. She cannot remember me from one visit to the next.

'Hello, Jean.'

'Oh my God. Have you seen me cats, love? Me mam stopped by earlier. I'm worried to death about me cats. I haven't fed them for two days.'

I know that this is not true for several reasons. For a start, Jean is too old to have a mum. Second, the ladies on this ward do not get visitors. You would think that relatives might want to visit, but the truth is that none of them have any. Being in Threeways for years causes you to lose touch. That happened to me as well.

'It's okay, Jean. Do you want to come with me? Perhaps we can have a look in the other room?'

Most of the staff are too busy at this time of day to spare any time for the patients. Talking time, that is. They are usually heaving patients on and off the commodes.

'Hello, Tim,' a voice shouts from inside one of the dormitories.

'Oh. Hello. Who is that?' I don't go in unless I get permission, because then it is safe, meaning that there are no ladies getting changed or washed or whatever it was they do to them there. The main dormitory on Ward Eighteen is a huge long room.

'It's Sue. It's okay. Come on in.' I like Sue. She is my favourite nurse on Ward Eighteen. She is always so grateful for our help, but all we do is make the beds in the morning.

The pungent reek of urine soaked sheets and shit from incontinence always makes me reel. When I look at a collection of pictures on the nicotine stained walls, they are feeble efforts done on the ward by hands that have lost almost all control. It is a sad sight.

'Good morning, it's always nice to see you lot.' Sue was about to wheel a freshly changed old lady out into the sitting area. 'Who's with you today?'

'Er, Mike and Sid.'

'All hands welcome. Like I say, it's good to see you. We can catch up later for a cuppa.' She pushes the wheelchair away, the occupant slumped forwards in her bright pink dress.

We set to work making the beds. We are regular visitors to this ward and so we are organised and work quickly. One person fetches fresh linen from the linen cupboard. The two others strip a bed. Then the first person removes the soiled linen in a laundry bag while the two others make the bed up again. It is well-rehearsed.

Mind you, it pays to watch where you venture on Ward Eighteen. There is a high risk of putting your hand in something that had been left behind by one of the patients. Mike once slipped on a pool of liquid. He got up to find a large dark brown and smelly stain on his trousers. There was another time when he opened a drawer in a bedside locker to replace a pair of glasses. In the drawer was what looked like a handful of

Maltesers. He made the mistake of picking one of them up. The chocolate turned out to be…well, not chocolate, rolled into a ball and placed back in the locker by one of the patients. Funny how it always seems to be him.

All of the ladies here are old, they get replaced by another when they die. A human conveyor belt. Still, there are familiar faces on this ward, like the woman who makes repetitive movements as if she is sewing. She might have once gone to OT, that place of craft, the world full of satin and buttons and weaving and sewing. I think one of the nurses told me the lady was once a seamstress, so perhaps before she was at OT she worked in the on-site tailor. Now, she sits and makes the repetitive movements with nothing in her hands.

I hear a screech. It isn't Mike.

'Help me,' it says. At first I am alarmed and wonder if I should investigate. 'Help me, will you.' I recognise the voice the second time and ignore future pleas. 'I'm wet, someone has made me wet. Help me. Help, help, help.'

It is Iris, another poor old lady, sitting in her own urine.

I feel sorry for the old ladies on this ward. They are lost souls, lost from the world and sometimes even lost from themselves. I also feel sorry for the nurses. They charge back and forth with armfuls of clothing or soiled nightdresses. They hook the ladies on and off the toilets. A nurse comes through from the toileting area. She wrestles with a dress, trying to fit what seems to be too small a size on to too large a patient. It is not their fault, the nurses. They do their best, but coping with all these old ladies, thirty-nine of them on this ward, it must be difficult when there are only three of you to manage.

I hope I never end up in a ward like this. I wouldn't want to be woken up early by the lights going on and the nurses drawing back the sheets letting the cold air in. I know that they take bowls of steaming soapy water with them. And a flannel. And a towel. I can only imagine how that must be as a patient who cannot express their feelings.

As for our work here, we take our cue from the nurses. We work hard on Ward Eighteen. When we finish, we go to the dining area for tea and chocolate biscuits. My suggestion is that one of the nurses brings them in as a treat. They are not hospital ones, none of the hospital biscuits have chocolate, so I think one of the nurses brings them in as a reward. I make sure to check the seat before I sit down. There is not a lot worse than feeling the warmth of freshly soiled seat.

'Another great job, you three. Don't know what we'd do without you.'

We finish the tea and leave. I am seen off by Jean, who greeted me on his arrival.

'All right, me love?' she says, holding the door open. 'Don't forget have a look for me cats out there. I'm going to have to get back soon. I'm expecting me mam in a bit.'

I stay with her as long as possible in case she decides to go off down the corridor. Goodness knows where she would end up then. Eventually one of the nurses has to come and rescue her and allow me to leave. As I do, I think about the remnants of the person that used to be inside that body.

When we get back, I see the familiar face of Tony, a patient from another ward. I have known Tony for years.

'Hello, Tony, we haven't seen you for a while.'

'Anthony, dear boy, Anthony.' He pronounces the 'th' like in the word thespian.

'Yes, of course. Sorry. How are you anyway?'

'Very well, dear boy, I am about to make an announcement.'

I watch Anthony placing a handmade poster on the wall of the day room. It reminds me of a notice I once saw in the administration area. It read:

*On no account are the nursing staff to solicit favour from any patient. You are not to exchange, borrow, lend or otherwise barter with any patient. Any breech of this rule will result in suspension or disciplinary action.*

That is humorous, you have to admit.

Meanwhile Anthony announces to anybody listening, 'I shall be giving a poetry reading in the Blue Room at four o'clock tomorrow afternoon.' The poster pretty much says as much with the addition of some colourful squiggles and shapes. Now he starts telling the ward that he is particularly fond of painting. He announces his desire to paint in the style of Mondrian. He described his poetry poster as a prototype for his forthcoming canvasses.

'I shall be making use of bright colours and bold shapes.'

Just as I think that I should give him some of my poems to read, and that I am the only one paying attention, I hear a snigger. Behind me is Neil. He is staring at us through his thick, food-stained glasses. His hair is greasy and swept across his forehead. Seeing him and Anthony together reminds me of the time when we had an art therapist in the OT department. I think I mentioned her already because Sid drew a graveyard. I cannot recall her name but she tried ever so hard with us all. This was despite the fact that we used to waste her paints by splashing them on the paper with no real idea of what we were doing. She suggested ideas and encouraged us to paint what was on our minds. What she failed to realise was that the mind of every mental hospital patient is a train. It calls in at despondency and moves on down the branch line through terror and anger to outright emptiness.

Neil did a monochrome depiction of the hospital grounds once. At first sight it looked chaotic, but when you concentrated on the shapes, there was something there alright. Although it resembled some of the abstract art in my favourite book, I was able to make out the main block. Also some of the paths and the outlying units of Threeways. He spent ages creating the images in what ended up being a work of ironic subtlety. I think he surprised the art therapist that day. He surprised us all that day. I knew then there was more to him than people assumed.

'Still want to go to the social?'

Neil nods at me. His face looks eager.

'Come on then, let's go. We still have time before lunch.' I go to the dorm and grab my coat. It's cold outside.

'I'm just off to the patients' club with Neil.' The nurse in the office nods but doesn't look up.

'Okay, Tim.'

'Off to the patients' club.' As he repeats my phrase, Neil's voice sounds more assured than earlier.

We leave the ward and walk through the long corridor. I take a special look at the doors just in case there is one that the old man found. All I see is the solid bolts, iron locks and the rivets of Victorian engineering. There are also the usual half-glazed entrances to the dentist, the porters' room and the general stores. These corridors seem to go on forever some days. I can stand at one end and stare at the endless receding passageways, with their arched ceilings and windows down one side. From some of them, you can look outside at the airing courts. In the late spring, the trees are fantastic, all full of leaf and surrounded by colourful flower beds. It's not that time of year yet, though, and the trees are still spiky and bare.

There was a time when I wondered if there was a part of the hospital, a place deep in the heart of the building, perhaps even in the cellars, where secret experiments were carried out. There is a lot of mystery here, even for someone like me who has been here all this time. And don't forget the underground reservoir with its millions of gallons. Who knows, perhaps the experimenters come and go without anyone seeing.

Neil walks alongside me, stooping, with his hands behind his back like an elderly headmaster, occasionally peering up at me as if to check that everything is okay.

'The social, Tim...it's run by the IT Department, isn't it?'

'No, Neil, it's run by volunteers.'

'Volunteers, okay.'

As we walk out of the entrance of the main block, that particular conversation seems to be going no further. There is some scaffolding opposite. There is also a man standing by a high ladder. He is staring up at the other end, scratching his head and puffing on a cigarette. It looks to me like he is figuring a way to get to the top. It occurs to me that I might have been a window cleaner if I had not been consigned to life in Threeways. I mean, I'm tall, so that would have given me an advantage, and I like the outdoors. Then the idea of water on cold hands on a day like today makes me shiver.

'Looks like we've got the builders in, Neil.'

'Builders, yes.' His brow furrows and he turns his head to look at me. 'Builders are swindlers, Tim, aren't they?'

That makes me laugh. I cough afterwards. 'Some of them probably are, Neil, yes.'

'My old dad, he said, he said.' The point is slow in being made, but Neil spits out the punchline with enthusiasm. 'He said don't put all your money in the banks.'

Quite what that has to do with builders is uncertain.

'That's okay then, Neil, because I don't have any money.'

This makes *him* laugh. I am glad because he looked anxious earlier on. We continue on to *Fags and Shags*, the fusty odour of stale cigarettes and centrally heated coffee stains greets our entry. I head for the counter to get the tea and Neil stays right next to me, his eyes scanning around the room.

'Go and get a seat, Neil.' He grabs my arm.

'Stay with you,' he says.

When I look up, I see that he has spotted a fracas on the far side of the club where two patients are grappling. They have taken a hold of each other's lapels and are both bending forwards as they cuss and swear indecipherable words at each other. It puts me in mind of the Goya painting of the conflict in the courtyard. Neil watches as the melee develops and quickly fizzles out. One of the patients turns and leaves the room, and the other sits back down. At the other end of the room there is a scruffily dressed man sat on his own muttering through a fog of smoke over a half-drained mug of tea. I have seen it all before many times.

'You'll be okay, there's hardly anyone here,' I urge. He nods and trots off.

As I wait for the tea, I watch a woman bend down to retrieve a half-eaten pie. It is covered in hair and dust, so she brushes it. Then she sniffs it. Then she opens her jaw and it disappears into her mouth. She walks past me, humming. Another woman is scratching her head. I recognise her as Scratchy Sally. She is always scratching. Her hair has bald patches where she scratches so much. You can see her nicotine-yellow fingers moving back and forth as she scratches another red patch onto her scalp.

As I walk to the table to see Neil, I spot him backing away from a large man, who has his back to me. It is the unmistakable bulk of Jack. He lives on a back ward with the violent men. Like me, he has been here ages.

I hear him saying 'Gimme.' Then, more urgently, 'Come on, gimme.'

'What's going on?' I ask. I look at his outstretched hand. It is ingrained with dirt, and there is black under his fingernails. I don't dwell on the thought.

Jack scowls at me. Well, I think it is a scowl, it is hard to tell as Jack has a squint. Nothing a trip to the Threeways optician would not sort out. I almost say this out loud.

'I said, what's going on?'

'Jack wants my fags,' says Neil, in a low, apologetic voice.

'Does he now?' I place the tea on the table and stand upright. As I do, I feel the pain in my chest, but I do my best to ignore it. 'Well, he's not having them.' Neil has the cigarette packet out already, and he has handed a couple to Jack.

'Jack,' I try and ensure my voice is clear. 'They are not yours. They are Neil's. Give them back.'

We seem to have developed an impasse, because Jack stares at me. His eyes are menacing, his frown deepening, but he doesn't scare me at all. I have seen too many Jacks over the years. I resist the urge to cough.

I now realise the reason Neil was edgy this morning. It also explains why, a couple of days ago, I caught him smoking five cigarettes at once. That is true as well. He had one between each finger and the fifth one in his left hand. He was puffing them in short bursts as if nicotine was about to be banned.

'They *are* mine,' says Neil, finding some courage.

'How long has thing been happening?'

Jack grunts at me. Neil shrugs his shoulders.

'Well, Jack, you can leg it.' I offer my thumb over my shoulder to emphasise the order. 'You leave Neil alone from now or I will come and see you. Do you understand?'

He doesn't say anything, but I know that he doesn't want my six feet two of mental hospital mass paying him an unexpected visit. He slinks off without a word.

I sit down and Neil grins. I start coughing and a red spit hits the table, which I wipe away with my sleeve.

'Now then, if he tries that again, you're to come and see me, right?'

'See you,' he says, looking at me through his mucky glasses. 'Right, Tim.'

'Good boy, now let's have our tea.'

Amongst the assortment of other patients who are in the club, smoking and drinking coffee, is Deanne, a little lady from Ward Nine. She barges past us and starts to rummage through the ashtrays for butt ends to smoke. She is dressed in an odd combination of green skirt and blue-checked tee shirt, mainly hidden by the red cardigan draped around her shoulders. Her greasy hair is falling every which way from beneath a faded headscarf and her shoelaces are untied on both shoes. A plume of grey ash is spilling down her top.

Neil decides to show his newfound confidence and snaps at her.

'Deanne! You shouldn't do that.' He makes a tutting noise with his tongue, and angles his head sharply to one side, peering over his glasses at me. 'She shouldn't do that, should she, Tim?'

'Er, no, Neil, she shouldn't.'

Deanne doesn't care. She turns her head to the wall. She is used to being told off for scrounging butt ends. Next, she places her left hand over her ear and starts whispering.

'Never mind, Neil,' I tell him, 'let's not worry about it.'

'Yes. Never mind.'

The two of us have our tea. The conversation persists as a jumble of thoughts and responses. Neil is happy.

'Jack is what upset you this morning?'

He nods.

'Well, it's finished now.'

Neil nods. 'That's a nice watch, Tim. It's solid gold, isn't it?'

I realise that he is back to normal. 'Er, no Neil. It's a cheap watch.'

'My Uncle John. He had a watch. He would work all day, bloody hard work, he used to say. My Uncle John, he was a coal man. Bloody great sacks of coal, you know. That's hard work that is, Tim.'

'That is hard work, Neil.'

My favourite art book tells me that Neil is the hospital equivalent of Manet at the fairground: swirling, chaotic, unfinished, but also engaging, mysterious and entertaining. His thought processes are never quite connected, like a Kafka novel.

We sup the remains of our drink, Neil stubs his butt under his shoe and places it back in the packet.

'Shall we get back then?' I ask.

He nods, and we leave *Fags and Shags* suitably refreshed, deciding to go back through the grounds the long way. When we go past IT, Neil admits that he doesn't like Mr Williams.

'He's a bully, you know.'

Of course, I agree with him.

'Nobody likes a bully,' he says.

Now I copy his habit of repeating the previous sentence.

'No, Neil. Nobody does like a bully.'

I am still thinking about Williams when Neil makes an announcement.

'Er, I just have to get going a minute.' Neil doesn't wait for a response, and his progress across the lawns is like a squid in the deep ocean. It is a strange movement. He disappears behind a large bush. I know what he's doing, because I have seen it before, so I wait. Eventually, he reappears with a smile on his face, zipping up his flies and putting his jacket back on.

With normality restored, we walk past the old chapel and up the lane by the right side of the main hospital block. We walk past the cabbages and carrots being grown in the gardens, while Neil keeps me entertained with more stories of the gardeners. As we walk past the OT department and the laundry, we see a van arrive. It isn't a delivery van. Well, not unless you call new patients a delivery. We pass the administration block, where so many bureaucrats are busy filing, noting and typing. We complete the tour by entering the main building through the side door situated by the pharmacy and walking up the long corridor. One hundred and ninety paces to the ward.

**(A haiku)**

*It rose half a tone*
*The sudden whimpering voice*
*That no one would hear*

# Chapter Nineteen

So here I am at Linnet House. It looks like a cottage where someone's granny might live. I am standing here waiting. Jan brought me from Ward One, she seemed to think I might get lost. She knows me better than that. I mean, I think I should know this hospital by now. I am the last one who needs the new road names they have suggested for the paths around the place. Another idea to make things sound normal. It seems a bit late to be naming paths when you are talking about moving people like me out onto the other side of the wall with the otherworlders. If they do that, there will be nobody left inside to walk about the newly named lanes. What will they do then? They will have wasted all that money on the signs.

Anyway, here I am, waiting as if I am about to be interviewed by Dr Metcalfe again. Ron's big idea, this is. I agreed to come and have a look because I didn't want to upset him. He is the coordinator, remember? I am to be a bench mark. A long-term patient a success? I never thought of myself as a success. But what will happen to Millie?

Upstairs, someone is hoovering. I once read a thing about that in the library. The man who invented the first electric hoover was called Spangler. He worked in a department store in America and had to beat dust out of the carpets. The problem was, he had asthma, so he designed a machine to suck up the dust instead. Then he sold the idea to a person called Hoover. I bet you didn't know that. I might be expected to Spangle the carpets if I am sent to live outside.

I almost laugh at the thought, but a face appears from around a corner. She actually looks a little like my granny. I am guessing at a high KQ. She is wiping her hands on a tea towel.

'Hello, Tim.'

'Hello.'

She is smiling at me. She seems to be waiting for me to speak.

'Don't you remember me, Tim?'

I have to admit to her that I don't. She says it doesn't matter. She tells me she used to work on one of the wards where I went when I first came in. That was a long time ago and I am embarrassed to say that I cannot remember it. There is probably reason for that. One that goes beyond the fact that we are both so much older and now she looks like a granny. I do not tell her that, though.

'Never mind, welcome to Linnet House. Come on through and I'll tell you all about us.'

Over a cup of tea, the nurse tells me that the patients here do almost everything themselves. I don't have such a problem with that, apart from the cooking, which terrifies me. I suppose it would make a change, get me out of that stinky dorm.

She is pushing a plate of biscuits my way. I notice that the ashtrays are not overflowing with butt ends. No point Neil coming here, then.

'Tell me why you want to come here, Tim.'

I consider making something up. I should have had a story ready. I didn't think about that. But then again, Ron did not warn me.

'Ron wanted me to come and visit,' I say. There, that puts the situation into context. 'I didn't like to disappoint him.'

'We would rather you were motivated to move here,' says the nurse. She smiles when she says the sentence. 'Would you like a cigarette?'

Would I? I take one out of the packet she points to on the table. 'Thanks.'

'We can talk about that stuff later, if you prefer. Many patients are uncomfortable not knowing what they are letting themselves in for.'

She is right there. The nurse gets up and starts humming and adds a log onto the fire while I finish the fag. When I slurp the remains of my tea and place the cup back onto the mug holder, she claps her hands.

'Good. Let's go and take a look around, shall we?'

The bedrooms are much smaller than the ward, with two beds in them instead of twenty. The lounge space is small, too. I see a lady with rosy cheeks and a checked shirt dusting a chest of drawers. She smiles at me and says hello.

'Are you coming to live here?'

'I'm not sure,' I say. 'Maybe.'

I notice the woman has big feet that make her look like a doorstop.

'It's nice here,' she says.

'We have eight clients here,' the nurse tells me, taking my arm and leading me on. Eight *clients*. That sounds like I am having a meeting with a bank manager or a solicitor. Not that I have had either of those, you understand. I wonder if I would get upgraded to client from patient if I came here. She tells me that some of the clients even do their own shopping. I am not sure I could cope with that.

She starts asking me questions about where I want to live when they let me out of hospital. I have no idea about that.

'Never mind,' she says again. We have a social worker who helps with accommodation.'

A social worker. Probably like one of the people who comes to the ward meeting on a Wednesday who wear leather coats and bangles. I hope he or she is more enthusiastic about finding places for people to live than coming to the ward meeting.

We pass a room that she describes as the laundry. 'We encourage our clients to do their own washing,' she adds.

'I have no idea how that works,' I say, trying not to make it sound like a protest.

'You'll soon pick it up,' she assures me.

It is not like the laundry place on our ward, that is only a cupboard where the sheets are kept. It reminds me of a time I saw one of the nurses coming out of there with the ward junior doctor who was working on our ward at the time. They were both red in the face and she was panting. Her hair was messed up as well and after she smoothed down her skirt she made an effort to neaten the wayward locks. The nurse started straightening his tie. They walked in different directions not saying anything to each other.

Remember what I told you about *Fags and Shags*? Well, I know the signs of sexual exchange well enough and it goes to show our standards are not so different to theirs.

At Linnet House, the nurse leads me into the kitchen, which is small but incredibly tidy. The plates are stacked in a wooden rack on the wall, the tea towels draped over the sides. There is a calendar on the wall with a picture of a ship above where the dates are.

There is another ten minutes of the nurse chatting. She is trying to assure me that life in Linnet House is an excellent stepping stone to a better life. Only, when she fills in the detail, I start to worry.

'We do our own shopping here,' she says. Just as I start to wonder what they shop for and why, she continues. 'Well, not *all* of it. But we make a list of what we need and then catch the bus into town.'

'What kind of shopping do you do?'

'Shopping for food, mainly.'

I must look puzzled, because she explains.

'You see, we cook most of our own meals here at Linnet House.'

I admit to her that I cannot cook for toffee.

'That doesn't matter, Tim. We can teach you.'

I thought she might say that, so I try my best to smile so as to not let on what I am really thinking. At the same time, I start to wonder whether that was why Ron took me to town, to test me.

'Anyway, talking of food,' says the nurse, rubbing her hands together. 'You must be getting back for supper.'

I thank her and make my way down the path. I close the gate at the end of the garden and turn and wave. As I rejoin the main drive, I see a black hospital cat. I say it is a hospital cat because we have a number of them at Threeways. They roam about and get fed from the scraps from the wards. And help to keep the rats away, apparently. Their existence is not so different. We are rabbits, mice, rats, cats, the beating breathing anonymity of related species. Black, brown, grey, red, orange, blue, if you like, the colour makes little difference.

On my way back to Ward 1, my thoughts remain on Linnet House and I decide that it really isn't for me. All that cooking? Let the younger patients have a chance. I mean, out of eight hundred patients there will always be someone else who could benefit. What I will say to Ron, I am not sure.

My trip is interrupted when I see Ray stooping near a flowerbed. He looks like he is weeding, but that does not seem like the thing to be doing in January.

'Hello, Ray.'

He turns and places a finger to his lips. Then he points to his hand. Ray has massive hands. I cannot remember if I said that already. He beckons me closer. As I get near, he opens his hand to reveal a tiny bird.

'Found this little chap,' he says. 'I don't think he can fly properly yet. He probably fell out of a nest. I'm going to put it up in a tree so it's safe. Yeah. Fabulous.'

I watch as his bulky frame works its way forwards until he reaches the trunk of an ash tree. He reaches up with an agility I would not have expected. His movements are so careful that his delicate passenger is never in any danger. He retreats from the tree as if he is walking on ice.

'Off you go, little friend.' He nods at the success of his mission. 'There. He's safe. Fabulous.'

'Yes, that is fabulous, Ray.' My eyes start to prickle as his humanity transmits an energy through the hospital air. 'Shall we go for lunch?'

'Lunch. Yeah. Fabulous.'

We walk back to the ward together. Ray spends most of the time chuckling to himself.

I am grateful that, even after all these years, there are people and things here that still have the potential to cheer me.

Ray Winters: High KQ.

### (For Ray)

*The quirk of madness,*
*Sends an imminent threat,*
*In a blur of the world.*

*But it fails to displace.*

*The smell of the gas,*
*And fear of the voice,*
*Warps the illusion of time*

*But it fails to displace*
*The goodness inside.*

R. I. P.

# Chapter Twenty

What was it PL? *Which way shall I lie to fall asleep?* The hospital buildings look heavy today. The stonework looks darker than normal. The sky is pressing down on us, buildings and all, like a concrete blanket or a wet overcoat. There is sleet. I always think that sleet is more spiteful than snow. Sleet hits you in the face like someone throwing grit. The air is cold as well. Today is like living inside a choc ice.

It was sad about Wendy. I never told you about Wendy, but she got run over and died.

### *One of my Poems (For Wendy)*

*Today, the sky is grey,*
*The trees are bare.*
*The leaves have fallen*
*Onto the ground.*
*The air sends a breeze.*
*The wind is not worried that the day is sad*
*And someone died.*

# Chapter Twenty-One

Dying happens, I know that. Most of us smoke ourselves to death. When a patient dies in Threeways, the fact doesn't get noticed by many people. The nurses might be sad if they had formed an attachment to the patient. But on the whole, it is another dead body and a passing statistic. When someone dies on a ward, they arrive with a trolley with a big steel cover like a metal shroud. I always think it looks like an upturned tin bath. The nurses have a ritual of covering the corpse with sheets. It is a solemn affair. Sometimes I think it is a shame that they don't reserve such respect for patients when they are alive. It is a shame when you have to be dead to see how nice people can be to you.

Nobody pays much attention when they are performing their death rites. It's another Threeways ritual. Most patients will be more concerned with what is left when somebody passes away. What will happen to their clothes? Did they have any ciggies left? That type of thing.

After the wrapping ceremony, they put the body onto the trolley and cover it with the bathtub. Then they wheel it out of the ward. Wendy didn't have a bathtub because she was run over outside of the hospital grounds, so I expect a normal ambulance picked her up. That was a few days ago now. I have been thinking about death. That's not a subject I think about a lot. The trouble is, when you are faced with the prospect of a new life, which is what Ron was talking about, you start to think about the one you might leave behind.

It could be worse, though. Sid talks about death all the time. He seems to look forward to his own passing. He is always asking for death to come and find him. It must be horrible to feel like that. Williams doesn't help any, I know that.

The line between life and death is a thin one, and the ghosts of old friends roam the hospital grounds. This is our kingdom, our domain, and when we leave, however we leave, we never really leave. We will be here for ever and ever. Wendy has probably gone to the eternity of space that I mentioned a while back. She already knows the answer as to what happens next. It could be nothing, but it could be that Wendy is looking down on us now, like patients of the past who are wandering the place of their former existence, looking over our shoulders and reliving a forgotten life. They might recall their private thoughts or their daydreams or their nightmares. At least they will be free of their numbed drug-induced earthly spirit. No more head fireworks for them.

The world keeps on turning, the doors keep on opening and closing and the colours of life continue to weigh on our days.

There is snow outside today. Like I said before, snow is not as nasty as sleet. It looks nicer too. Through the window is a grey ceiling and a white floor covering.

Even in this weather I see the people arriving for the ECT clinic. They look glum and anxious as they plod their weary way around the back to a single-storey building which his run by Sister Bridget. They used to do ECT on the wards. They would bring a white-coloured machine with wires out of the back. I don't know why they didn't simply ask us to poke our fingers into the electric sockets. I had ECT for a while. First your head gets filled with lemonade, then the fizzing grips your brain. Then a skewer goes through your skull. Then fury. Someone has put a motorbike in the room, the revving is unbearable. The hounds of Hell tear at you. Encased in cement, rocking like a demented infant. Finally, your backbone is stripped out through the top of your head.

I never knew what it was for. I don't think the doctors knew either as they only ever said things like 'It will help you get better', and 'it is for your own good'. When you are about to have electricity put into your head, you might like to know why. All I remember is the fear of getting onto the bed and having to bite on a piece of rubber. Looking up, surrounded by white coats, you have no idea whether you will have a broken limb or simply a raging headache after. The nurses used to say, 'It will be okay, Tim'. How could they possibly know? I won't scare you with any more detail, but most times, I was left feeling worse rather than better. When you wake up, you have no idea where you are for a while. And the throbbing head feels like there is someone inside punching their way out. Perhaps they thought it would take our minds off all the other problems we were carrying about.

Whoever looks back at this place, the sociologists or historians or alien species looking in, they will be like the archaeologists of today viewing the ancient peoples of Peru. Those who pre-date the Incas, I cannot remember what they were called. The future inspectors of the past will look at this system and shake their heads. They will ask how so many people were herded into a man-made receptacle and managed there for decades at a time. 'These people must have lived here,' they will say. 'What?' says another, 'all together? It's not possible.' 'Yes,' says the first, 'it was like a community.' 'A very strange one, I should think,' says the second.

Yes, it is true, we are the ambassadors of the mad and we will be studied for our contribution to stoicism. Perhaps they will see us once again, as people did in the past, as special.

Over the far side of the day room, I watch Neil scraping about in some ashtrays. The butts are spilling out like maggots from a festering wound. He lights the dog ends and sucks the life out of what remains.

## AMBASSADORS OF THE MAD

*The plague of the mad, feared scourge of the minds of the healthy – spreading unstoppable, virus-like, represented in ourselves like the figures over the archway. We are the acolytes of lunacy, the Bedlamites of moon-motivated madness.*

*The vibrating, shaking, drooling, dragging, shuffling,*

  *Scuffing and huffing*

   *Scarred and jarred*

    *Crying and dying*

*Laughing at the night.*

*Hamlet, Lear and the mad Lucia.*

# Chapter Twenty-Two

Dear old Ron. He has been away on holiday and he has come back full of enthusiasm. I haven't told him my feelings about Linnet House yet, mainly because he has not mentioned the visit. I do feel a bit bad about deciding not to go. I fear that Dr Metcalfe will be pleased and Ron will be disappointed. So for those reasons, I am leaving it as long as I can.

Today Ron is enthusiastic about the jazz selection he is playing. Ray the Bird Man seems so as well. He is sitting very still and upright as usual, staring ahead at the wall. His face, which is rosy and shiny, looks like that of someone who has received fantastic but unexpected news, disbelieving but elated at once.

'Jazz. Yeah. Fabulous!'

'You like jazz, Ray?' Ron seems pleased to see some support for his group selection.

'Yeah. Jazz.' He nods and pauses. 'Jazz. Fabulous.'

That is that then. Ray likes jazz. In truth, Ray likes most things. He likes his food. He likes the gardens. And now I know he likes jazz. Mostly, though, he likes his food.

Before we start the music, I make my suggestion to Ron about the musical instruments. He thinks my idea is great. It is great. We are interrupted by Marjorie, who is grumbling almost inaudibly.

Neil decides to intervene. 'You know, Marjorie, if you sit *there*,' Neil emphasises the last word by pointing to the seat of her chair, 'if you sit there, if…' he is getting to a point. 'If you sit there…' he points again and the pace of his speech increases as he gets to his apparent punch line '…you get an extra cup of coffee.'

'God! What the hell is he talking about?'

Neil laughs. Edward sighs. Ron intervenes.

'Don't worry about Neil, Marjorie.'

None of it makes sense and Marjorie stares back at Ron, producing a growl of hostility. Her throat rumble is like a V8 engine.

That is Springhill social life for you.

'Bastards!'

Ron leans over and places his hand on her arm.

'What's up, Marje?'

'Fuck off.'

I know he is not about to fuck off. He has heard it too many times before.

'Tell me, Marje, can I help?'

I know immediately that this is a silly question, and I suspect Ron already knows what she wants as well.

'They won't give me any more fags.'

Ward Nine is obviously withholding Marjorie's cigarettes.

He asks her if she was naughty. It is another stupid question. She's not going to say yes, even if she did upset a couple of the poor oversensitive nursing staff.

'Well,' she says, 'they wouldn't let me have my fags so I shouted at Sister and tipped the milk jug over at breakfast.'

'You know that you can't win a fight like that.' Ron's voice is understanding.

You see what I mean about how situations get interpreted? Why does Marjorie get the blame for being provoked? It's all about perceptions, and ours are not the same as theirs.

'Tell you what,' says Ron. 'I'll give you a couple of fags. But try to be nice when you get back to the ward or they won't change their minds. You know that.'

Marjorie's chin has grey hairs like metal spikes. The battlefield remains of Agincourt, perhaps? Or Ishandwala; the spears and arrows of the exchange, discarded and ready to be ploughed over by later agricultural machinery. The nurses on Marjorie's ward might do the same to her whiskers with a razor acquired from one of the male wards.

She smiles at the upturn in her personal circumstances. She takes the gift and, having achieved something positive, she leaves the room.

'I'll say adios then.'

He knows he has bribed her, we all do. In fact, Edward even tells him as much, and it is probably against all the therapeutic rules. But what are a couple of fags if it makes her happy?

Like me, Marjorie has been here forever. I know that she had a baby once and it was taken away. That is why she is in Threeways. Having a baby when you are not married was not thought of any a good thing back along. It sounds stupid now, but that was back then. She isn't the only one. There have been a lot of ladies here who got admitted for the same thing. People sometimes say a baby was a mistake. In Marjorie's case, it was a mistake she has suffered her whole life for.

'You're a good man, Ron.' Having seen Ron hand out his fags, this is all Edward says. Then he goes back to the book he was reading.

Ron starts the music. The soothing guitar and sax samba rhythm creates a relaxed atmosphere. Apart from the brief interlude with Marjorie and the cigarettes, everyone is mellow. In fact, it is unusually quiet. To my surprise, Neil finds it in himself to sit and listen. Even Sid is smiling. Well, I think he is. It could be a grimace.

The needle winds its way back and forth on the disc like an exotic dancer. I watch as it moves slowly to the middle.

After the usual post-music chat, the scramble to leave the Blue Room would make you think there was an unexploded bomb under one of the chairs.

Ron takes the record from the turntable and gives the shiny black disc a wipe with his arm before replacing it in the sleeve. He switches off the record player and starts humming one of the tunes. I don't think he realises I am still in the room.

'Ron, could I have a word?'

I was right, because he jumps when I say it.

'You gave me a start, Tim. Sure. What's up?'

'It's Mr Williams at IT…'

Perhaps I shouldn't bother involving Ron. He is a nice bloke and I don't want to get him into trouble. In any case, abuse is nothing new here. I've seen so many people forced to take medication. I've seen people jabbed with injections, beaten and kicked. Arms get twisted. You can't object directly because they say you're uncooperative. We are not allowed to speak up or we get more of the same stuff.

Once I remember seeing a woman get thrown onto a bed. I saw it from across the hall. It wasn't in Ward One, but I saw it. She was sat on by two big nurses and another pushed an injection into her. She screamed, but they laughed. That was mean too.

'What about him, Tim?'

'Huh?'

'What about Mr Williams?'

I had forgotten that we were talking about Williams.

'Well, he's mean to Sid.'

'Mean?'

'Yes, he hits him and shouts. I know IT is important, but he can't...doesn't defend himself.'

I hope I have not gone too far. It is hard to tell from Ron's face, it is staring at the floor. 'I see.'

He goes quiet again and I hope again that I have not created a problem I can't undo. I trust Ron, though.

When he answers, his tone is reassuring, and his voice is calm. 'Leave it with me, Tim.'

I watch as he replaces the record on the shelf. But do you know what? As much as I would like to think, he will sort our difficulties, it seems unlikely.

## High Hill

*A chamber of tears,*
*Produce the season of fears.*
*Cold walls of doubt*
*That will never get out*

*Over our high hill.*

# Chapter Twenty-Three

I was right to be doubtful, because I see from Williams' face that Ron's visit was not successful. Williams seems to be more spiteful than ever today. There is a different feel about staff violence. I remember Terry, a patient who used to drink a lot. One night, he snuck a length of wood back from the woodwork shop. I guess he must have carried it down his trouser leg, or inside his coat. Anyway, he was so fed up with the snoring of the bloke in the next bed that he smashed him over the head in the night. Wow, I bet that was a rude awakening. It was bad enough for me, just hearing the shouting and screaming. Terry was moved to a secure ward after that. The other bloke had stitches and a headache. It didn't stop him snoring.

That is different from what Williams does. Violence between patients happens. It happens all the time at *Fags and Shags*. People are always jostling with each other, but that is a consequence of being in Threeways. Throw a lot of mixed-up patients together, give them drugs and not much enjoyment, and they will find a reason to argue.

Tommy is here today. He laughs a lot. On his ward, he stares at the floor and laughs at his feet. Tommy would laugh if his head was on fire. It really annoys Williams, which is not hard, as you know. Tommy laughs at things that are not there. Tommy stares at the floor and laughs. When he is here at the Box Shop, he laughs at the bench. It irritates Williams, which is not hard, as you know. Like I say, Tommy stares at the floor and laughs. When he is here at the Box Shop, he laughs at the bench. He might be laughing at his voices, or things from another universe, who knows? What I do know is that Williams likes to control the place. But he can't do anything about Tommy, except tell him to shut up, which normally makes Tommy laugh even more. Williams has been trying for ages to get Tommy moved from the IT placement, saying he is 'disruptive'. Tommy only comes here once a week now, and Williams has been told it is the best he can hope for.

Anyway, what's disruptive about being happy?

Things settle when Williams gets annoyed and disappears to his office for twenty minutes. I find myself hoping he has had a heart attack. You know how I associate people with creative works? I find it hard to imagine Williams as a painting or a piece of music. His ugliness does not deserve to be validated by beauty.

Are we not punished enough in this life by having to reside in Threeways? This further trial seems to sneer at us and compress our patience to an increasingly smaller space. If God really created the Earth in seven days (or was that six?) why would he cause men to be so cruel? Why would he place others in a position of torment? And then again, perhaps Ron is an emissary from a distant part of the universe, sent to save us all with his plans. Ron the Saviour.

I complete yet another box and add it to the pile in front of me when I spot Millie waving at me from outside, and my own heart warms. She is probably off to the laundry, that is her Box Shop. She goes there to fold sheets most mornings. They don't use the mangles any more. They used to have massive wooden pulleys, and baskets all over the floor for putting the clean laundry into. The female patients working there used to wear long skirts and little frilly hats. I used to find them quite attractive. Before that, Millie worked in the needlework room, but her eyesight is not what it was. Now, she sometimes gets to work in the ironing room. She tells me likes that.

Sorry, I was telling you about spotting Millie. Anyway, the moment I have forgotten seeing her, she appears in the unit. Her face is beaming.

'Millie,' I say in a hushed voice. 'What are you doing in here?'

Her face drops and she looks down at her shoes. I feel as if I have told her off. She is wearing the blue dress with the white stripes. Her hair is neat and she has on lipstick. She also has a small brooch pinned to her chest.

Before we have any further interaction, I sense his presence.

'What are you doing here?' Williams' voice grumbles. The entire workshop falls silent.

Williams starts forwards. He is pointing his finger at me. He walks around the bench, and I see his eyes are wide and his temples are throbbing. The pencil falls from behind his ear. Then he points at Millie. She is fiddling with her brooch and staring at me.

'What are you doing here?'

He has repeated my question twice, but it sounds far less friendly. He turns and asks me. 'What's she doing here?' I see him grind his bony hand into his palm, his jaw clenches and he hisses through his teeth. 'She's not supposed to be here.'

Well, I already know that, that is why I tried to get her to leave.

'She's just leaving,' I tell him.

'Coming in here, disturbing my workforce, chattering, slowing things down. You can't come in here.'

Williams' voice is rising with every word. I can see the muscles in his neck harden and his arm seems to be twitching. I am starting to fear for his health. No, I am starting to hope he does have a seizure before he does anything to Millie. He is capable of that sort of behaviour.

Before he gets the chance, I push Millie in the small of her back and she takes the cue to scurry out of the department.

'Leave her alone,' I hear myself almost shout the words. I realise that I am in trouble, but I want to protect Millie. You understand, don't you?

I watch Williams. His face gets redder, and his eyes narrow. I hope for a moment for his sake that he doesn't close his jaw any tighter because he will need a trip to the hospital dentist if he does. Veins appear in his head. Did I tell you he was bald, by the way?

'Get out!'

He screams the words at me and I think the inevitable is coming. I cringe and anticipate the impact. Instead, he turns on his high heels and limps back to his office. He slams the door and a pane of glass shatters. The glass tinkles onto the floor.

I stand for a moment and I wonder why he has not attacked me.

'Tim,' a soft voice pierces my trance. I look up to see Sid waving me towards the door with all nine fingers. 'Get going before he comes back.'

I don't need a second invitation, and I clear out of the Box Shop as quickly as I can. I didn't want to leave Sid in there, not with Williams in that type of mood, but I look over at the clock tower and it indicates twelve-thirty. So, that means it is twenty-five past twelve, and five minutes to the end of the morning shift. My hands are shaking as I light a cigarette and take in the smoke. I can still feel Williams' shouting pulsating in my ears. The tension starts to evaporate with the deep breath.

I feel a tap on my shoulder, my immediate thought is that Williams has followed me out. When I turn around, I see Millie. Just when I am about to repeat the question about why she was at the Box Shop, she holds out her hand. In it, there is a parcel wrapped with brown paper and a blue ribbon.

'Happy birthday,' she says, and she reaches up to kiss me on the cheek.

Did I tell you it is my birthday today? No? Well it is. I am fifty-three years old.

### On Being Fifty-Three
### (Please excuse me, PL)

*I'm here, you see*
*And I'm still me,*
*The seconds pause*
*To record the scene,*
*Of what has passed*
*And went between.*

*A silver streak,*
*A golden seam*
*Revealed in life*
*By a humble dream.*

*The boy I recall,*
*Headed the fall*
*Onto the rocks*
*With anguished blame.*
*I could not help*
*The man I became.*

*And now I see,*
*At fifty-three*
*Offered the chance*

*In life that remains*
*To carve out hope*
*And diminish the pains.*

# Chapter Twenty-Four

Between coughing fits, I was thinking about the head fireworks and it struck me that there are two types of innerworld. There is the place we live, and the other place where some of us retreat even further. You know, there was a time when people who heard voices used to be special, like they had a particular power and everyone thought they were getting messages from God. That changed along the way. That is strange because some of the patients in Threeways *do* think they are getting messages from God. Perhaps they are. Like I say, life is a funny thing.

You remember my theory about experiments being done in the hospital? I am starting to think I am an experiment, and I wonder if Ron's idea is for his own professional curiosity or my benefit, I haven't worked it out yet. He was talking today about work. I think I already told you about the jobs I once thought I could do. He made it sound a little like IT, but without the bully Williams. I am unsure about working for a living, though. One thing I do know is that the more I think about Ron's plan, the more my brain works on the pluses and minuses. It also throws up so odd thoughts that have never occurred to me before. One of them spurred me on to make a list.

## List of Things I Have Not Done: by Tim Cavendish

- Travelled on a plane
- Got married
- Gone to France on holiday
- Watched a proper football match
- Gone fishing for the day
- Had a real job
- Been to Sunny Prestatyn. (That's for PL.)

I am afraid that my life is not an interesting one in the conventional sense. You can see that from the list. I could also say that I have never been to New York and seen the Statue of Liberty. I have never watched wild geese fly over the frozen wastes of Canada. I have never seen kangaroos in Australia or the giant redwood trees in California. I have read about them in the library, and to me that is good enough. All these things are stored in the same place as my knowledge of famous writers and composers, ready for me to call upon at times of need. As for the idea that I experienced hardship, it might look like that, being stuck in Threeways for the majority of my life, but I have known some kind people. Of course, I could point to the things I have done, like written poetry and stories, but that is a much shorter list.

You can read one of my longer poems, it is called: *In The White Room*. It is not exactly *The Iliad*, but I am proud of it.

For the remainder of today, I am going to take it easy. There is no Box Shop to worry about and no beds to make on Ward Eighteen. I would go to the library but it is closed today. The lady that normally runs it is off ill. I know how she feels. I don't even feel like delving into PL today. Instead, I am going to behave like the staff expect mental patients to behave. I am going to sit about chain-smoking and staring at the ceiling.

# WhiteRoom

# Chapter Twenty-Five

## *In The White Room*

*The White Room; hostile isolation. In the White Room is power fizz and crackle. Dull, snow-blind emptiness. Howling, hissing, sometimes pissing. Waiting, forever waiting. And listening, guided by the Helmsman devoid of foresight. The blind Lookout shouting backwards. All the time ticking. Long, short, quick slow. Seconds tick somewhere else — fixing attention on another place.*

*Into the hole, the Ethereal Highway. The missing orb, the absent sun. No moon in this milk flavoured sky.*

*Record the detail on the long-play memory — looped into feedback riddled frenzy. Filters use the weblike tendrils of the brain, showing the mist of yesteryear. Quiet is the enemy of sanity.*

*Lifting eyes raise the gaze to see nothing but the wall of white. Hunger, thirst, all usurped. This is the sea of emptiness, the quarry, the unfilled grave. The crooning soul offers apple tree branches, reaching out from the summer vision to combat the cold.*

*Skull scraped clean of flesh, hollowed out. Yet more white pain is forecast. Muscular weakness, and breathing crushed by a ton of benign matter.*

*Echoes of Purgatory because Paradise is lost. The Hellenic majesty, the olive groves on Mount Olympus, the green grass of*

218

*ancient lands that cannot be seen from on high. Hover over the Lookout, watch into the swirling hiss. After, sleep-deprived by animal sounds, the gnarling, growling, snarling, snapping – teeth, jaws; saliva dripping gums. Sometimes stained black claws, the pulling Griffin, the pecking Raven, even the coiled Mamba. Today it is the Snow Beast.*

*Clumsy hands trembling. Cover the ears to protect the rising wave of noise. Dynamo whirr. The Lookout signals a breach. The Snow Beast released, crossing icy waters, slopping in and out, leaving oversized drops to cascade and explode inside a bony cranium.*

*The elements of Earthly Concern, the smiling Ship of Fools. An empty church receives no prayer.*

*The Messenger stealing through the windowless mass of white, via icy passages, subways with flowing rivers beneath a frozen table top. Pain shooting upwards through teeth and nasal cavity and traversing the brow. Through fibres and vessels and nephrons and axons and into the cortex.*

*Crouch. Keep small, the Snow Beast will pass, closed eyes mean things don't exist – but the sounds suggest impending snarl. Waiting, listening. Waiting and watching.*

*Thousands of years of tragic visions wasted – jettisoned into the trash bin of forgotten experience. A feather, suspended in a summer current, turns to flapping, floundering, breathless uncertainty.*

*The mind's eye, searching for a sun-soaked lawn in lazy August, where dying figures are given up to the worship of Helios. Then a blot in the eye, a bullseye, a red noise and a creeping silhouette — the disciples of the Snow Beast flitting here and there. Darting, piercing, injurious nicks of time. A silent scream into the white night.*

*Ossification. From the shadows arrives a rolling, rumbling, baying agony, overtaking individual anxiety, swarming with white darkness. The Lookout is redundant.*

*A hand on the shoulder, a push to the direction of the seabed. Harsh crashing rocks contained in flesh. Revolving tremor, the Snow Beast and the howling mania. Respond with a yell or a dribble. Then the quiet.*

*Fear, pain, fear. More fear. Laughing, mocking, funny, amusing, humorous danger. No peace even in silence.*

*Flat calm is the water of endlessness. The Spirit lies coiled, the waves passed as invisible radiation and the Snow Beast has gone away, sated after the Feast.*

*Open sky, the clank and yell and creak and white light that mingles with blue.*

# Chapter Twenty-Six

My eyes are sore. I couldn't get out of bed this morning because of my cough. My chest feels someone has placed that old iron roller on my ribcage. It feels as if I am in that painting by Fuseli. *The Nightmare*, I think it is called.

Luckily for me, Ron is working this morning, else I may well have been tipped out of the bed for being lazy. I wonder whether the soreness might be due to the hassle we had with Williams yesterday. I was coughing a lot after that.

Yesterday evening, I went to the ballroom with Millie to watch a film, so perhaps that was it. We didn't make it to the end of the film because I was coughing. The ballroom is so massive that the sound echoes about. The chatter in that room swirls about like a thick fog of voices. I didn't want to spoil the film for my fellow viewers, and it was quite busy. Millie said she didn't mind, but I think she did because she was enjoying it.

I am tired. The coughing kept me awake. I hope I did not disturb the others too much. I never realised that it goes surprisingly quiet in the dorm. I watched the torch of the night nurse on her rounds flash around the room, but after a couple of checks, she must have given up and gone to sleep. They are not supposed to do that. They would more than likely be sacked, but they all do it. It doesn't bother me, as long as they are there if anything serious happens. Apart from my coughing and the creaking from the old building, the rest of the night was nothing but darkness.

Ron has organised for Doctor Cooper to come and examine me, I am lying in bed, staring at the cobwebs on the dorm ceiling, watching the ward move around me. Now and then I drift off to sleep and get woken by the sounds from the day room. I can hear a woman visitor from another ward telling people that she is in her sixties. 'I've been in every mental hospital and clinic in the whole of England. I was in a secure place; the last place was a secure place. I didn't need that did I, luv? I can't understand why they put me there.' Her rambling continues. 'And then there's my sister. She steals things from me she stole some books. She's more mentally ill than I am, it's just that she's always got a man in tow. She's an alley cat and she's more mentally ill than I am. She knows a German, a Nazi.'

I am not sure who is listening, probably nobody. She will be told to return to her ward in a minute. 'And I know a priest who is a friend of mine. Well, he's not a friend, more of an acquaintance. He told me that. He can help and that's because I don't trust the Mormons. I don't like them; I go to the church round the corner here. My friend Judy picks me up. I don't know if she's coming this week she might not be able to.'

The voice tails off until all I can hear is the clanking of cutlery of the plates, the chairs scuffing in the dining area. I can smell the burnt toast, drifting through from the kitchen. I lie in my bed aching. There is a metallic taste in my mouth.

'All right, Tim.' It is Mike. 'Want me to play you a tune?' He has come to collect his guitar before setting off to OT. He always takes it there, not so much to the Box Shop.

'Thanks, Mike, but probably not, if it's all the same with you.'

The thought of him twanging right next to my bed makes my muzzy head tremble.

'Okay, hope you get better soon. See you at lunch.'

I watch as he leaves the ward. I think that perhaps if I had been lucky enough to have had a brother, I might have liked him to have been like Mike. Sid is more like a cousin: a distant figure who I want to know but do not fully understand. I feel for Sid and he gets little to cheer him. Me and Mike tell jokes when we are together with Sid to try and make him laugh so that he feels better. Mike always forgets the punchlines. I watch Mike sling the guitar over his shoulder and bounce off. It was kind of him to offer to play me a tune, he has demonstrated his KQ. Not that I ever doubted it. I envy him the trip to see Mr Jackson.

My eyes feel heavy, but not as heavy as my chest. The feeling of rawness when I cough is made worse a dozen internal razor blades. These are sharper than the useless ones I shave with. I can feel that the iron roller is not budging, setting up residence, ready to be overgrown by the tendrils of my weakened lungs and remain there until rediscovered in the future by a wandering madman.

'The doctor is here.'

Through my dozing, I hear Ron's voice. I open my eyes and expect Dr Cooper, only it isn't him.

'Who are you?' I ask.

'I'm Dr Webb.' He sounds irritable. 'Sit up, please.'

I drag myself onto my elbows and further out of my sweaty sheets.

'Further,' he commands, sounding every bit as rude as before. I consider him to have a low rating on the KQ scale.

I feel rough. It is like he doesn't want to be here, or perhaps I have disturbed an important part of his day. As he leans over me, he looks distracted. I can smell his breath, which tells me that he hasn't had time to clean his teeth.

He is not nice, but mentally I have to thank him, because he inspires me. I think I will write a story about him and his kind, how they don't understand. By the way, I am not the only one who writes things down. There is a woman on Millie's ward who keeps a notebook and writes down every interaction. Most of it doesn't make sense. Well, not to me, anyway, I am sure it does to her. I suppose it is her way of making sense of her existence, of working through the day-to-day happenings.

I am jolted out of my thinking by the doctor prodding my belly.

'Does this hurt?'

*Of course it bloody hurts*, I want to say, *you're prodding me.*

'Any pain?'

'A little, in my chest.'

I see a pustule just above his collar, reddening along with his razor rash.

'Breathe,' he commands.

I breathe. Then I cough. He has his knee on my mattress, and he doesn't look too happy about it.

He tells me to open my mouth and he sticks a wooden thing that looks like a lolly stick in it. I try not to cough any green sputum over him.

He stands and smooths his jacket, replacing his stethoscope around his neck. I am relieved when he turns to Ron and tells him, 'It's just a chest infection'. He could have said that I had pneumonia. Or TB, then I would have to go to the isolation ward, only that's now full of alcoholics. I must admit, though, that I lied. It was only a little lie. When he asked me how long my chest has been hurting, I said a week. In fact, it has been about a month. Maybe more.

When he leaves, I ask Ron if I should get up. He tells me to stay in bed and he will get a student nurse to bring me a cup of tea.

A little later the tiredness catches up with me and I drift off.

I find myself wandering the main corridor in Threeways. Only, in the dream there is lots of light and it doesn't smell of floor polish and sadness. Because it is ajar, I stop at the door marked, 'Tailor'. It is two thirds of the way along. Or a third, if you are coming from the main entrance. I push the door and go in. There is nobody there. The door closes behind me. The dark, wood-panelled walls are shiny. There is a thick carpet, which makes it seem quiet. There is a desk, with a leather surface, on which are some pins and an oversized pair of scissors. My curiosity takes me to a curtain, a changing room. When I go in, there is a tinkling noise as if someone has entered a shop. The mirror does not reflect an ageing patient, the tall one with the bad cough and the messy hair. It shows me a blue sky and sand. I reach out and the distant cry of a gull grows louder as I feel drawn through the mirror.

The other side is endless flat beach, sunshine and light, warmth on my skin. The smell of the sea goes up my nostrils. It is a long way from crumpled cigarette butts and tasteless soup. My body floats and floats, and I don't bother to question the effect. In the distance, I see an old man sitting on a rock. His head turns to face me and even from far away I can see he is smiling. I start towards him, I want to know how he got here, and what he does. A gentle breeze touches my face and I walk light footsteps, barely making an impression in the sand. The feeling is exhilarating, the expectation invigorating. I walk closer and the man smiles. Then waves at me and he is gone.

I awake to the cool of the flannel mopping my brow. The nurse smiles and asks me if I am feeling all right.

### He Cares
### (For Ron)

*I am here, I am me,*
*He is there.*
*Is it wrong, by the way,*
*That he cares?*

# Chapter Twenty-Seven

Millie has come to see me on the ward this morning. She wants to make sure that I am feeling better. I am, so we both sit in the day room having a cigarette. Millie has the habit of lighting a new cigarette from the dying butt of her previous one until they are all gone. I have to remind her to slow down. I look at the plants and they look like they need watering. That is because Jean the domestic is on holiday and nobody else bothers. I will do it later. We are listening to the radio, and Millie is tapping her foot to the music. She doesn't come to Ron's group; I don't know why. Mind you, I have never suggested it. Perhaps I will.

Dr Metcalfe is in his office with Dr Cooper and a person from a drug company. I saw them going in together. They are obsessed with new drugs here. I can always tell when they have been to see him, because I start to hear new names read out when the nurses are doing the medicine round. I am pretty sure that these men bribe the doctors. On their desks, they have pens and mugs and other items with the names of the drugs on them.

What they care less about is the people on the receiving end. Us. The side-effects give us headaches or problems with our weight. They also make us restless. I see patients twitching and hopping, even when they are standing still. Their faces contort into weird expressions, and the dribbling is uncontrollable, despite what they tell us.

Millie and me decide to get out for a walk. We pass Mad Geoff, who is wearing a green bobble hat, and he is shouting at the wall of the main building. He doesn't say things like Martin, that he is going to call his solicitor, or sack the superintendent. That is not really Geoff's style. Instead, he is shouting to the small windows on the second floor.

'I can see the reach of the gasses and the heat.' He starts to laugh. 'Don't worry, I've been frightened before, so don't go telling me it's all about the cigarettes. I know what a modecate injection does. There was a flash of green and suddenly my leg hurt. Then my curtains flew open and my brain flew away.' He starts to do a dance as if to celebrate his speech. Me and Millie wave, and Geoff waves back and grunts at us with a smile of recognition on his face.

I do not know what madness really is, but I know places like Threeways make a special type of insanity in people. You end up behaving in a way that is different from normal but a different type of normal. I have seen it happen to hundreds of patients. We have a different code here. There really is no point in taking a microscope to the ways of our world. That will be the job of those who examine our legacy, the ones who will shudder at their revelations. The beings who move about in this human chess game will be revealed as a subject of interest. But let's leave that to the future generations.

Halfway along the side road leading to the cricket pavilion, we meet the Caribbean nurse I know vaguely from around the grounds, I think his name is Valentine. He hasn't been here long. His parents are Jamaican immigrants who came to England in the fifties. He is always complaining about how cold it is here. He says that his country is a place of clear skies and sandy beaches and endless sunshine. In fact, I do not think he lived there for all that long, perhaps a few years as a child. But it goes to show how difficult it is to leave your home.

I look at his dark shoulder-length hair in tight curls, and his moustache. He always wears jeans with his white nurse's coat. They are not supposed to, but he seems to get away with it. Somehow it suits him. He's normally escorting a giant woman from Millie's ward which makes it hard to see who is leading who.

'Hello,' says Millie, in her squeaky voice.

'Are you late for work?' I ask him.

'No, man. I'm scouting for Carol. Have you seen her today?'

'No, sorry, we haven't.'

Carol is also from Ward Nine, by the way.

'Curses! Uncool. She went off the ward a while ago and you know she shouldn't go out alone.' We already know that. 'She'll never know where she is.' We know that, as well. 'Okay, I have to split.'

He walks on a few paces and turns around. 'Hey, do you want to walk with me, you two? I'm only going to be looking for Carol.'

'Well,' I say, 'we were going to the social club, but we can leave it for a bit and go the long way round.'

'Cool!'

He says 'cool' a lot.

We walk with him as he continues on his search for the missing patient. Valentine asks me what my ward like at the moment.

'Same as ever, really' I say. What was he expecting? They really do ask some odd questions at times.

'Uncle Sam still there?'

'Of course. He likes being head nurse of the ward. It's what he knows best. He is like the rest of us, glued to the walls of Threeways.'

He chuckles at this.

'Have you any idea where Carol is?' I ask.

'No, man. I look all over by the top by the ward and that.'

'Sometimes she goes down towards bottom wall,' says Millie.

'She's right,' I say. 'Sometimes when I am at the social I see her walk past the window and down to the gates.'

'Cool, man. Let's try down that way. It's as good as any, and I'm not having a whole deal of luck. Sister will pan me if I don't find Carol. She don't like having no bother on her ward, man.'

We know that as well.

Carol can barely communicate past a couple of words. Catatonic, that's how some of the nurses describe her. But that must only count for certain times, because I have seen her loads of times in the grounds with her bouncy semi-skipping but determined walk. It is funny because she keeps her arms straight down by her side like she has been lassoed, and she doesn't move her head. It is a little like watching a penguin. I have no idea how she sees where she's going. She has a habit of sneaking off the ward, particularly when the double doors to the airing court are left open. She walks out and if she is not spotted by the ward staff, she will keep walking and she can end up almost anywhere within the grounds. Or off them. When it is discovered that she is missing, a member of staff is sent out to make a search. Like Valentine.

We walk across the cricket pitch. In the summer, the smell of freshly cut grass from this place fills my nostrils. After spring, it is one of my favourite times in Threeways. The evenings are so long and we get to enjoy the grounds. Sometimes I meet other patients from different wards and we have a smoke, or we go to the social club. Apart from the occasional entertainment laid on by the hospital, that's about it.

Valentine's eyes are scanning around all the time, like a nervous bird, hopeful that he might see Carol. We walk around the back of the pavilion, towards the tennis courts and the social club. Just as we pass the south entrance gate, Valentine stops instinctively and turns to face the road outside. Beyond the road is a row of hedging and beyond that was a local golf club.

'I'd better leave you now man. I gotta feeling about this one. You carry on to the club, okay?'

'Okay, Valentine. I'll see you again soon.'

'No sweat, man.'

We wish him luck and watch him walk out of the gates and over the road into the dusty car park, which is dry and full of loose stones. Despite the cold, the sandy dust kicks up from his shoes as he walks towards the golf course. I watch as he pauses a moment and scans again.

I have seen occasional adverts in the local press about 'escaped' patients. They are hyped up, of course, intended to sound more dramatic than they really are, in an effort to induce fear in the locals. That is not difficult, by the way. People seem to be naturally afraid of the mad. I don't know why. We are pretty harmless on the whole. I often think you have as much chance of being bashed over the head in the town as in Threeways. But you can't beat a good scare story.

It is ironic that they used to try to keep us all locked in and now they are kicking people like me out. When I look back to how things used to be when I came here, I would never have thought the opposite would happen. Ron was talking about a social worker who finds places for patients. I really don't know about all that, what with the murder and bombing and kidnapping they all get up to. The people outside, not the social workers.

Me and Millie turn back and go to the social club. Inside, a man I don't recognise is standing at the counter wearing a flat cap over some a white covering.

'What's under your hat?' Millie has asked the question before I have a chance to think about the situation.

'Cotton wool.'

'What's it for?'

The man replies that it is to stop people stealing his knowledge. At least it is not tinfoil. It is usually tinfoil. 'If I let them have my ideas, then they will know what I'm thinking. The authorities are always trying to get my secrets, the cotton wool stops the thoughts getting out.'

Head fireworks. Like I said before, we often get that type of talk. I wonder whether the ideas are self-perpetuating, like any regular stereotype. He didn't mention radio transmitters. Like I said, we often get that type of talk. He seems to think the transmitting is being done by his head.

I am making it sound funny, it is a habit you acquire around here, because things like that happen all the time. In some ways it is amusing, but I have seen some sad sights here when patients get tormented, when their brain turns on them. I remember watching a patient bash his head with a stone to force his voices to stop. That is not a happy sight, let me tell you.

Millie nods and turns to the serving lady. 'I'd like two cups of tea, please.'

That's Threeways for you, we carry on no matter what. I sit at a table and she comes over, slopping tea into the saucers. She puts mine down on the table and lifts up her cup so that she can tip the saucer contents into it. Only she doesn't. She drinks the tea directly from the saucer. Now I giggle. It's not always bad here.

The man with the cotton wool hat sits on an adjacent table and starts humming. When I get talking to him, he tells me he was transferred to Threeways from another mental hospital. He also tells me that he is a multi-millionaire with various life threatening illnesses. The first part I might believe, the second part I do not. But you never know.

I nudge Millie as I spot Valentine, who is walking past the window. He has grabbed Carol's arm and put his hand on her shoulder, guiding her forward. Millie giggles. Valentine has removed his jacket and has put it around her. I guess she was naked again. I forgot to tell you that she takes her clothes off as she walks around the grounds. It doesn't matter about the weather, she does it every time. And she is not the only one. Remind me to tell you about Paul one day.

### *The Night Spirits*

*I hear the approaching darkness, the cold, dense blanket of the night.*
*The early hours bring the dead zone*
*and the reclaimed souls of those who have been and gone.*
*The rhythm switches to a deadened acoustic,*

*then the animal sounds from around the grounds.*
*The howling fox calls out, the rats busy themselves,*
*scavenging for what they can get.*

*There are distant spirits whispering from an ethereal kingdom.*

*These ghouls are sent to play with our expectations,*
*sometimes burrowing into our sensibilities,*
*our frailties, our insecurities.*
*We are weak, defenceless creatures,*
*Powerless to resist.*

*Eventually the spirits are replaced by the surging power of the*
*pipes,*
*the flexing muscles of the awakening beast,*
*the flow of energy.*
*The creation is rumbling a warning*
*to all who care to listen.*
*The assured solidity with which the world is reclaimed*
*overwhelms the fleeting reign of the dark.*

# Chapter Twenty-Eight

I know I said the woman who runs the Occupational Therapy Department is an idiot, but we really don't mind it here, me and Mike. Mr Jackson is a kind man, and he is helpful, not at all like Williams.

Mike is looking forward to finally finishing his magazine rack. It is going to be the longest projects in the history of Threeways Asylum. I can't fault his enthusiasm, though. Apart from his guitar, he used to collect stamps. He had pages and pages of them in various albums. He had a whole drawer full of little clear bags crammed with stamps from all over the world. None of them were valuable, but he liked to collect them. Then there was the time he had model soldiers all over the place. He had a great big battlefield full of French and English infantrymen dressed in red and blue. They were all set up to look like they were a real battle scene, with tiny cannons and flags and everything.

Mr Jackson is helping me with the sanding today. Halfway through the morning, he brings in a tray of tea. He lets us have a break and he also lets us drink our tea by the benches. We all share a joke. Can you imagine that happening in the Box Shop? I can't.

Mike just has the varnishing to do and he is finished. I am starting to get excited about his project coming to an end. Today he has been filing and measuring. Usually he does this with his tongue poked out of the side of his mouth is concentration. Now, he has stopped. He stands back to admire his work for the day. There is glue running down one side, and he wipes the excess away with his thumb. He then rubs that on his trousers. His concentration and attention to the detail are impressive. As is his enthusiasm.

'Nearly finished?' I ask him.

He nods back and sticks up his gluey thumb. 'Just the varnishing.'

'Well done.'

'But I'm saving that for the next session. Mr Jackson has told me to let the glue dry, and he says I need a clean space when I varnish. I'll do it next time.'

If that were me, I would be rushing to finish it. I can't help but admire his patience. I will use Mike's magazine rack. As long as Ron is still speaking to me after I become a let-down as his project focus, I will get him to take me into town. Then I will buy some magazines to put in the magazine rack. Mike would appreciate that.

When we are about to leave the department, Mr Jackson calls over to us. Well, not to us. To Mike.

'Will you play for us, Mike?'

Mike sniggers as if he is having his leg pulled.

'I mean it, Mike. I would like to hear how you are doing. It might warm us up on this cold January day.'

'Really?' Mike looks like he has been offered a knighthood.

'Really.'

'Well,' says Mike. 'Er, well. I *could.*'

'Come on then, let's all sit around the bench.' He directs Sid and me and a couple of other woodworkers to sit. 'You prepare yourself, Mike. I'll be back in a bit.'

I ask Mike if he is okay.

'Bit nervous.'

'You can do it.'

'Yeah,' offers Sid, puffing on a cigarette. 'Come on, man, you're gonna be great.'

Mike balances the guitar on his lap and strums, as if tuning up in an orchestra. He plays a chord or two and his shoulders loosen.

Mr Jackson reappears with a tray of tea and some cake. 'Come one then, let's all sing along.'

It is not exactly a singalong, because Mike's progress is what you might call steady. It doesn't matter, because there is foot tapping. And Mr Jackson is making percussive noises with a screwdriver on the edge of a varnish pot.

I look over at Sid and he is smiling. I knew we would cheer him up. He loves music, so no more rubbish jokes without punchlines.

Mike claws his way through three tunes and repeats them without any discernible improvement. Like I said, it doesn't matter, his spirit wafts about the department and we all get drunk on the fumes.

When he is done, we all clap. I am trying to work out whether it is Mike or Sid with the biggest grin.

Eventually we leave. Mr Jackson was right; the weather is chilly but clear. We walk down past the laundry and the chapel and the main building with the pavilion on our left. That reminds me of the cricket matches. It also gives me the chance to tell you about Paul.

Every year, the staff organise a cricket match with the nearest mental hospital. Last year's match was hilarious for two reasons. First, the argument, second, Paul's guest appearance.

The Threeways vs Oldfield cricket match is held in July, in the same week as the hospital fete. The finance administrator at Threeways is a man called Reginald. He is the one who arranges the matches. He, he has a brother at Oldfield he liaises with. It's funny that such an English game is run by Reginald. He is a fat Welshman with big ears and a double chin. His body is like a beer barrel. His brother, Huw, on the other hand, is mild-mannered. He is senior porter at Oldfield Hospital. He is taller than his brother but just as wide.

On the day of the last match, the weather was perfect: a yellow disc in a blue sky. The pitch was bone hard and the grass had been cut into stripes by the hospital gardens staff, who had also carefully marked the square with white lines. They might have used one of the new rollers, I'm not sure. Remember the old iron one I discovered? That had long since retired. For want of something better to do, we all wandered down from the ward to watch,

As umpire, Reggie put on his white coat (there is no shortage of those at Threeways) and a floppy hat; he picked up the bails and went to the middle. The teams were mostly staff, but there were a few patients.

Some could bat a bit; others ran around after the ball. Some just sat around in the outfield enjoying the weather.

We watched and clapped enthusiastically where we thought we should. For a long-term patient at Threeways, it was always something different. Some patients fell asleep on grass, the rest of us smoked fag butts and rested. Our head nurse was bowling when Paul made his appearance.

The first sighting was his large gut and skinny legs, which I saw running towards the middle of the field. Paul was a patient from Ward Eleven, and he was naked. His arms swung as he raced toward the wicket. His greasy hair was stuck to his forehead and his face showed a fixed determination. Through his thick glasses, his eyes were focussed on the stumps. The players watched as he reached his target. Having a huge barrel of a body, Paul was not built for athleticism. With a shuffle and a hop, like a land-locked walrus, he jumped, but as it was more of a feeble little skip. He failed to make it and crashed in a heap. Paul was well known for his streaking. He would get out of the ward, take off his clothes and fold them in a neat pile by a tree. Then he would strut around naked until someone in authority came and put a stop to it. The psychiatrists had characterised it as 'attention seeking'. Paul got the thrill from the fuss that he caused. There seemed to be little that they could do about it.

The incident caused little by way of attention apart from laughter. This is a mental hospital, we see stuff like that all the time. In fact, we even clapped. Paul was rescued by a nurse who then took him back to the pavilion, that being the nearest place of shelter. He was ordered to remain there while she fetched his clothes from a nearby tree. The she got him restored to his pre-naked state of attire. Paul never made any fuss once he had been apprehended.

I don't know a lot about cricket, but it seemed to me that once Reggie said you were out, that was it. Not so. When Huw was told by his brother that he was out, he refused to go. There was a huge argument. The brothers stood belly to belly, shouting at each other. Perhaps it was deep-seated resentment, perhaps it was sibling rivalry, I don't know. All I know is that the head nurse had to intervene. Now if that was us, the whole thing would have ended in a swiftly administered injection of tranquillisers.

I am still not sure who embarrassed themselves the most. We all had a laugh though.

Back on the ward Mike wastes no time telling the nurses about his musical performance at OT. Even the head nurse listens carefully.

### *Garden*

*A winding path,*
*Where nobody goes*
*To a rusty gate*
*That nobody knows*

# Chapter Twenty-Nine

Remember I said I would write a story about the unsympathetic doctor? Well, I did. Here it is, I hope you like it.

*The shrill ring of the alarm rouses him from his slumber and he practically falls off the couch.*

Shit! Why do they always interrupt my break?

*Dr Webb silences his pager and lifts the phone to call in. He listens to the voice at the other end and kicks the table leg when he hears the request.*

*'An admission, doctor.'*

*'What? Another one?'*

*'Yes, sorry, doctor, we were only expecting the one, but this man is an emergency.'*

*'Emergency? In this place?' His tone suggests sarcasm. 'Okay, I'll be over presently.'*

What a dumping ground. How did I get stuck here? *Webb repositions the internal hospital phone receiver onto the cradle, rubs his tired eyes and huffs. Two admissions to York ward in the morning, after an on-call night that did nothing for the beauty sleep.* Shit. This is shit! *He rises and stretches, groaning as he does. He straightens his slim tie and runs his fingers through his hair; he eases his way into his white coat and wedges his stethoscope into the side pocket.*

*'Where is he then?'*

*The young nurse looks startled; she had not heard him*

*enter the ward.*

*'Hello again, doctor,' she says. Her breezy tone is not reciprocated, countered as it is by a furrowed brow. 'He's in the lounge.'*

*The medic stares at her with darkened eyes, his greasy hair has still not been washed. He has a reddening spot above his collar.*

*'I'll just go and get him.'*

*'Would you?'*

*Webb exhales deeply as he replaces the nurse in the office chair. The leather seat pad is warm. He looks at the wire in-tray; there is a row of textbooks on the shelf to his right. Psychoanalytic therapy does nothing for him. He lights a cigarette and inhales the smoke deep into his lungs. It rests there for a moment as he allows the chemicals to infuse into his bloodstream.*

*He rubs his eyes again as he picks up the man's case notes. Not the first time he's been here then. The file is stamped in black ink:* "Harrington Mental Hospital". *He opens the cover, unscrews the top of his fountain pen and starts to write.* "Medical exam: 25th January 1965".

I hate this job: the late nights, the cold early mornings the idiotic nurses, the incessant demands. And then there are the patients: the dribbling, shuffling, stinking mess of useless inhumanity. The hospital is a jumble of store cupboards, toilets, bathrooms, dormitories and cold, dark corridors. And ashtrays, loads of ashtrays, full of butts smoked down to the end. This place is a receptacle of wasted life, stowed away in nicotine stained walls.

*Webb flicks his cigarette ash onto the floor. His shiny brogue shoes react to the tremor sent from his leg and he grinds ash into the wood. He places the pen on the desk and massages his temples.*

*A stooping figure appears in the doorway. Beside him is the nurse.*

*'Here he is, doctor. Mr. Timmins.' She tips her head towards the patient and tells him to say hello to the doctor, which he fails to do.*

*Webb looks disdainfully at the diffident patient.*

God. What a mess.

*The smell of body odour and stale urine reaches him from three feet away. The examination will necessitate poking and prodding. He knows that he will have to put his hands on the grubby skin, stare into the grimy ears, and peer into the oral cavity reeking of halitosis and cigarettes. The thought does not appeal.*

*His gaze moves to the nurse: starched white cap and dainty smile. A small fob watch dangles above a pert breast. He wonders about the firm flesh concealed beneath the clean blue uniform.*

How many more of these hopeless individuals will they bring me to examine? They keep on coming, an endless stream of dross and misery. Worthless and aimless, their lives contribute nothing. At least this place keeps them corralled, away from the rest of society so we don't have to look at them. I can prescribe enough pills to keep him quiet, whatever he has done to get his sorry soul in here. I don't want to be coming back here every ten minutes because he has threatened a nurse or punched through a window and slashed his wrist. It's all about keeping the imbeciles docile, and that's what the drugs are really for.

*The nurse starts to tell the doctor about the patient's illness; that he was found wandering the street in a confused condition. He threatened the policeman who approached him. Webb simply stares at her.*

*'That's what they told me, doctor.'*

*She continues, conveying detail about depression, lack of work, vagrancy.*

The little nurse is blathering on about the patient's uncaring family. I'm not interested whether he was a teacher or a coalman. I don't care what bleeding heart tragic string of events rendered him so helpless. He's here now. He's now one of the numbers, one of the pathetic refuse that is consumed by the straining walls of this institution.

*Webb stubs out his cigarette and stands. The chair squeaks on the floorboards as he nudges it with the back of his knees. He looks at the nurse and indicates through to the examination area. The pretence of washing his hands seems futile in view of the task that faces him.*

*The patient is now lying on the examination couch. His feet are wrapped in filthy rags. His trousers are held together at the waist with string. His phlegm stained coat is missing some buttons.*

Before long, he will be ignorant to all this, blissfully unaware of his situation: where he is, how he got here. If I give him enough drugs, there is a chance he will even forget who he is. I will be doing the poor bastard a favour.

*Webb takes a pinch of cotton material between his forefingers and lifts the man's off-white shirt to reveal a grey midriff. He presses the softened belly.*

Nothing particularly remarkable. He probably hasn't eaten in a few days.

*The patient fails to respond when questioned about this. He also says nothing about whether there is any pain. This leaves Webb to make a guess from the non-verbal cues such as absence of wincing and squealing as he continues to probe. He tries to get his fingers to touch without touching.*

One day, I won't have to do this anymore. I'll be promoted to the consultant ranks and spend my days like the rest of the elite. I'll teaching juniors and publishing papers. It's a means to an end, Webb. Just remember that.

*The blue case file lies on the wooden table beside the couch. Webb scribbles some notes onto the page he has dated. Squiggles appear, detailing information about reflexes, condition of his abdomen, the yellow appearance in the whites of his eyes.*

How the hell did I get myself into this? Stuck in a mental hospital is not where I thought I would be by now. The only fun to be had in here is chasing some of the nurses. The process of dealing with the likes of this creature is at best tedious. Look at him, lying there. It's pathetic. Another one for the farm.

*'Is everything alright, doctor?'*

*The nurse reappears. Her clean looking face is a pleasing counterpoint to the state of the man on the couch. Webb peers at* it, noticing the gentle curve of her lip, the faint line of forbidden mascara, almost hidden in the fold of her eye.

'Fine. Can you fetch a cup of tea?' Although it sounded like it, the flat tone makes it clear it was not a request.

The nurse asks the patient how many sugars he would like.

'Not for him, honey. Me.'

He seems pleased to observe that she reddens slightly before apologizing and wandering off. A glow of manly pride warms his chest. He screws the pen lid back on and places it down beside the notes. He turns reluctantly back to the patient.

'Almost done.'

The statement is automatic. It comes out before he is aware of it. He wonders why he bothered, the man is not responsive, either too stupid or too ignorant to reply.

Here is the bit he has been dreading most of all. Webb picks up a wooden spatula and leans forward as he asks the man to open his mouth.

The stench is disarming. Webb takes a small step backwards and holds his breath, ready for another look. The area is swollen, he thinks, it is hard to tell, what with the pustulent deposits clinging to vascular putrefaction. Certainly infected. The teeth are rotten stumps sprouting from decomposing gums. He is reluctant to do it, but like any other doctor, he asks the man to say "Aah".

The mouth opens wider. The noise gargles from the angry red membrane, the breath sending out a poisonous gas.

There is a sudden whooshing sensation, and a frothing, fizzing splutter that builds to a rush of sucking flap air. A drain? Perhaps a strong wind outside? Webb is still peering into the mouth, unable to avert his stare, he looks deep into the

251

*cavernous space, past the tongue and the tonsils, past all the pieces of anatomy that he spent so much time learning at medical school. His ears are filled with the cacophony. He feels a strange pull, an irresistible power. The noise gets louder. He is drawn into the void, past the soft palate and the uvula. He is sucked inward, dragged by an inexorable force. Screams and howls sound, and he hears a cracking noise as his ribs tighten and his body is compressed.*

*Suddenly, everything is black.*

*When light is restored, Webb is dragging himself along. He feels the weight of suffering. The effort makes every action painful. He looks down. He sees a phlegm stained coat with missing button that envelops his frame. He sees his ragged feet sliding along the ward floor as he walks. He sees the grey skin covering his fingers. His breathing shallows, his brain is filled with a dense panic, he wants to yell and yet he cannot speak the words aloud.*

What is this? Hell. What's happened to me?
*With difficulty, he moves his heavy head, trying to make sense of his transformation. The smell of decay fills his nostrils.*
Shit! Where's that nurse?

*There is a dark voice, from where he cannot be certain. All he hears is the inquisitive tone:*

*'How does it look, doctor? How does the world look now?'*

# Chapter Thirty

The weather doesn't look too promising, but Ron seems determined to get us out. I feel like we are taking part in one of those war films where the POWs make a mass breakout. Ron is the chairman of the escape committee.

Ron possibly sees the trip as another practice run for his project. He will be able to go into the ward meeting and argue with Dr Metcalfe and the head nurse about how capable I am. Or he might be wanting to prove that we don't all run amok at the first sign of being let out of Threeways. Of course, he might just want a day out.

When he turns up with the minibus, I see Claire is with him. I think we are going to have a good day.

To my surprise, Sid agreed to come. I think I might have told you that he doesn't like to go out. Agoraphobia. I cannot remember the last time he left the hospital. Mike is with us. He is smoking a pipe today.

'Gone off cigars?' I ask.

He cackles and removes the pipe from his lips, letting a cloud of smoke escape from the corner of his mouth. 'Fancied a change,' he says. The smell of vanilla fills the van as we drive off. The picnic is already packed, courtesy of the main kitchens. All the musical instruments are safely stored.

Before Ron even starts the engine, Marjorie's growl starts. But she is not complaining about the ward, or lack of cigarettes. Her attention is focused on another matter.

'Oh my God!' she says. 'What's that smell?'

'Oh, it's terrible.' She is now wafting her hand in front of her nose in disgust.

Ron and Claire look at each other. Ron sniffs under his armpits.

'It's not me Marje,' says Ron.

'It's only pipe tobacco, Marje,' I say.

'No not that, I mean the awful smell of floor polish.'

The members of our outing look at each other inside the minibus. Marjorie sniffs and directs her head towards Mike.

'It's my aftershave,' Mike admits. 'I got it for Christmas, do you like it?'

Marjorie, who is usually so grumpy, actually laughs.

'Have you tried Old Spice, Mike?' Claire asks. 'It's all the thing. You can buy it in Boots.'

'Uh, erm, no. Maybe I'll get some and Marjorie would like that instead.'

'You can only try, Mike,' says Ron, who laughs as if he is not convinced.

We edge our way down the hospital driveway, past Linnet House and out of the main entrance. Ron turns to Claire and gives a cheer which seems to signify his surprise that he has passed the first test of the day.

The drive takes about forty-five minutes. Edward reads for the whole time and I watch out of the window, looking at the passing houses, then the fields. I have Millie by my side and she is happy just to snuggle up to me and say nothing.

During the journey, the visibility deteriorates because of the cigarette consumption inside the minibus. By the time we arrive, nobody can see out of the windows for smoke.

We drive through some gates and into a park, where I notice there is a large tent. Ron tells us that they are holding a music festival, which comes as a surprise. When Ron parks the minibus, we all pile out. We are a ragbag assortment of ill-fitting clothes and dented minds. Marjorie is complaining. Mike's pipe is not lit, but he has it clamped between his teeth anyway. Sid stretches. Edward nods to himself, smiles, and straightens his bow tie.

'Try and stay close by,' Ron says, as if we were children.

I know he doesn't mean it like that. He has taken responsibility to get us all back in one piece, I suppose. If he lost someone, he would have to explain the situation to the head nurse, and the last thing the head nurse wants is a problem. He would have to fill in paperwork and that would stop him looking at the newspaper or chatting to his friends on the other wards. We can't have that.

As you will have gathered, contact with the otherworld is still rare for most of us who have been in

Threeways for so long. I told you about the summer fête, where people from the town visit, some out of curiosity, some through a misplaced sense of civic duty. In the end, it amounts to the same thing: they all want a look at the odd folk behind the walls. There will be more trips like the one I had with Ron. And with places like Linnet House and their shopping expeditions, I suppose being stuck in the hospital will be more a thing of the past.

Claire is wrapped up in a coat with a furry collar. She is sweet. She is asking Marjorie if she likes Ron's music group. Marjorie isn't interested in replying. She has a short attention span. Anyway, she wants another fag. I am surprised that Ron has not told Claire about the group. If he had, Claire would already know that Marjorie comes to scrounge cigarettes. Claire should have gone to Edward; she would have got a more sensible reply.

We go and sit in the deckchairs and listen to some jazz, some poetry readings and a mix of folk music. We have blankets for our knees. Millie is happy. She is holding on to my arm and rubbing it up and down.

'This is a nice place,' she says.

It is nice, she is right. It is a bit like the music group without the dense smoke filling the Blue Room. I chuckle and Millie frowns at me. We stay like this for twenty minute, but Ron knows we are not a group that was going to stick together for very long and he is ahead of any splintering. He has thought about it, and I admit it was wise to send Claire to get some cups of tea, which she is now placing on the table. As she does, the skies are getting darker.

I watch Marjorie spend most of her time wandering about the field smoking. I know the reason for this is that she has extra cigarettes. She will smoke them one after the other until she has none left. Then she will come back and ask Ron for more. This is all fine until the rain starts spotting. She ignores it, despite Claire's waving and Ron's calling. She simply grins. The rain gets stronger and heavier. Even when the downpour soaks her, Marjorie stays out. She keeps her head buried into her shoulders. Her smelly shoes are getting wet. Eventually, Claire goes to rescue her, and she holds her coat over both of them. Marjorie is bedraggled but unconcerned. Her main worry is her inability to reignite the end of her sodden cigarette.

Inside the tent, I notice that Sid is nodding to a man with a Bob Dylan lapel badge. Edward has struck up a conversation with an elderly couple who seem interested in what he is saying. All I can make out from Sid is, 'Ronnie Scotts,' and, 'influenced by Charlie Parker, apparently.' The couple are nodding at him. 'Art Blakey on drums…etc…Chet Baker's trumpet playing. His was a tragic life, heroin addict…etc.'.

Quite how Sid knows all this is a mystery, but if I know about Sophocles and Manet, then why shouldn't he know things as well? It is possible that we have both spent too much time listening to Edward. Or Sid has been in the library when I haven't. The folk music is interesting, but Neil interrupts Ron, he needs the toilet.

I am struck by his approach to the problem. It is clear to me that if we were back at Threeways, toilet accessibility would not be an issue, thanks to the open grounds. Yet, even Neil seems to recognise that we are in a public place. He is hopping from one leg to another, looking like he is about to burst.

Ron asks, 'Are you okay, Neil?'

'Not really, Ron. I need the toilet.'

Ron rolls his eyes and casts about the field. He spots the toilets to the side of a small refreshment building.

'Come on then.'

Neil laughs and they set off, Neil skipping at Ron's side.

Later, I am sitting with Ron, we are eating the beef sandwiches prepared for us by the kitchens. I try and keep the conversation going because I am fearful that he might mention his pet project again. I do think about it, of course I do, but I have no idea what will happen to me. Part of me thinks I take a swig of the fizzy drink. It looks like urine in a bottle. It tastes sweet, though, so that reassures me it really doesn't matter.

I am enjoying the smell of the dampened grass when there is a break in the concert, if you can call it that. On Ron's instruction, our group heads to the minibus to retrieve the musical instruments. We all grab a piece and set off for a corner of the field, away from the tent.

We are soon all settled, and looking at Ron.

'Okay,' says Ron, 'here's my plan. I have this metronome,' he says, holding the item aloft, 'does anyone know what this is for?'

Without delay, Neil offers an answer. 'It's for hitting Marjorie.'

'It's for keeping the time of the music.' Mike announces.

'That's right. Mike.'

'Right I'll set it so that we have a beat to try and stay to.' He allocates the rest of the instruments. 'Okay, are we ready?' Ron sets the metronome going.

The clanging, bashing, rattling frenzied din is a spontaneous expression of fun. I look at Neil, who is staring out of his smeared glasses, grinning and giggling. Marjorie is concentrating for once on something other than a cigarette. Millie is bashing her own triangle with indiscriminate rhythm. Sid is smiling, and that is always a rare sight. There is no sense of timing, no organisation, no structure. But I feel as if I am part of a special moment. I probably should not say this, but sometimes I love my mental hospital.

The plan was for the group to swap instruments several times throughout the session. As it turns out, Marjorie gets fed up of the tinging noise she is making with her triangle. She throws it onto the floor and walks off.

Sid keeps a surprisingly good beat, whether he has the cymbals, the snare drum or the bongos.

Neil is standing by the side, rattling a tambourine. The only instrument that did not get swapped was Mike's guitar, as you might expect.

Ron asks, 'everything okay, Edward?'

'Er, yes thank you Ron,' he says.

'Are you sure? You look a little lost.'

'Well, I wonder if you might have a flute,' says Edward.

'Oh, I almost forgot.' Ron fetches the flute from his bag. 'There you go, is that any good?'

I watch Edward take hold of the instrument and hold it in his hands like he is holding a newborn baby. A smile appears on his face; he looks like he has bumped into a long lost friend.

When he plays, the cacophony being generated by the rest of the group falls silent. Like a lone voice, rising above the tumult like a songbird high in a tree, a trilling melody gradually makes us stop. It seems as if the lightness of his playing temporarily sends collective relief all the way back to the spinning minds back at Threeways. We all stare at him. When he finishes, there is spontaneous applause from the entire group.

I had no idea about this special ability. Nor, it seems, did Ron.

'Edward, that's amazing,' he says. The words are an understatement. We are all amazed, in fact.

'Oh,' he says, when he finishes the piece. 'It's nothing, really. I used to play in an orchestra.'

We sit and listen to him play another tune until he removes the flute from his mouth and we all start clapping again. Edward bows to us. What a thing it is when people surprise you.

Ron says that there is nothing more to do but pack away and head for a pub.

It is a good idea, as it turns out, because within ten minutes it is raining again. The pub idea seems risky, what with all that medication washing about, but Ron seems confident.

Our welcome is a warm one. In a quiet corner, we eat pie and chips and drink beer.

'Cracking day, Ron,' says Mike, who has rested his pipe on the radiator beside him.

'Very enjoyable,' adds Edward, who is clearly the star.

'Very enjoyable.' Neil reiterates the point for emphasis, laughs and then takes a swig of beer.

Marjorie has taken herself over to another table, where she is smoking. The scowl on her face suggests it may be her last cigarette. I am pretty sure that Ron or Claire will find another one. If not the trip back home will be given over to grumbling from behind the driver.

After leaving the pub, we get into the minibus and Mike starts singing.

'We all live in a Yellow Submarine...La la la la la.'

It was a great day. I don't think the antibiotics the doctor gave me are doing any good, because the pain in my chest is still there. I didn't want to say anything to Ron, not today, we were all having too much fun.

## Dropping

*Shadows of fear fall from the edge*
*Silver light behind layers of*
*Superstition causes*
*A white sheet to bring dark*

*Drop, dropped, dropping...*

# Chapter Thirty-One

'Where's Mr Jackson?'

'Not here.' Williams' voice is gruff. He looks even more pasty in the bright lighting of the woodwork department. He scratches his head behind his ear. I don't know why Mr Jackson is not here, as Williams doesn't elaborate. But seeing Williams do that, my first thought is a strange one, it is that the pencil he keeps rested there will come in useful for woodwork.

There is an air of disappointment mixed with tension. I can feel it without looking at the others.

'Come on,' urges Williams. 'Get on with whatever it is you idiots do up here.'

Any hope that Williams might be different outside of the Box Shop is wiped away. My guess is that we won't be enjoying our bench-side cup of tea today. This is such a contrast to the trip we enjoyed with Ron and Claire. I suppose you could say that it typifies Threeways life.

I cannot remember the last time Mr Jackson missed a woodwork session, but I know they sent a student nurse to sit in with us. We had a laugh with her as she didn't know anything about woodwork. That's not to say that the female nurses are not practical, because I have had a lot of help from them over the years. I have learnt about tying knots and playing card games, and bandaging wounds.

What a shame that Mr Jacksons' replacement this time is not someone nicer. When I look over at Mike, he isn't moving, as if the disappointment is still registering. I gesture to him with my head. He snaps out of his daydream and rests his guitar against the wall by the radiator.

Williams has found himself a high stool from where he can command an advantage over the rest of us. Like I have been telling you, Threeways is all about control.

Sid looks the most concerned, of course. He is sitting next to me, so perhaps this might help, especially after I stood up to Williams when Millie dropped by. I can only hope. I spot Williams topping up a coffee from a small bottle. He can't go into his office, where he thinks none of us know about his secret addition addiction, so he hides the bottle in an inside pocket of his jacket. Mr Jackson wears brown coloured overalls, splattered with paint and glue, to protect himself. Williams doesn't see any reason to wear overalls, he has no intention of helping any of us out here today.

Mike is in a private world, he has opened the tin of varnish, as Mr Jackson had instructed. He hovers the brush above the tin, as if enjoying the drama before he dips it in. He knows that this is the start of the end for his project. I am sure that the magazine rack will be the pride of the ward. Ron has been following Mike's progress reports with great interest. He says that we will put it right next to the television, so that the whole ward will be able to see it.

Mike's brushstrokes are methodical, surprisingly so. He applies the varnish with great care. It is funny, but I feel a sense of pride watching him. I miss the smell of vanilla from his pipe. Williams has forbidden smoking for the morning.

As usual, when I start coughing I try to prevent it by holding my hand and then my hankie firmly across my mouth. But that makes things worse. Williams looks at me with mean eyes; eyes that have narrowed. He has a great ability to produce menacing faces. I decide to go outside and, with the handkerchief still over my mouth, I point to the door to indicate my intention. He nods and turns away.

Outside, the air is cold. I look at my hankie and see the spots of red. I wipe my mouth and take a couple of breaths before the inevitable refrain. In the break from the coughing, I hear shouting coming from inside the department. I realise that, like an old lawnmower, Williams has spluttered into action. Poor Sid. I decide to go back in.

Only, when I re-enter the room, it is not Sid at the centre of the commotion, it is Mike.

'You fucking imbecile!'

Mr Jackson always tells Mike to maintain a steady brush line. In following these instructions, Mike has managed to move the varnish jar ever closer to the edge of the workbench. The inevitable has happened and now Mike is standing with the brush in his right hand. There is a distraught expression on his face.

'Idiot!' Williams is furious. Mr Jackson would probably have laughed. 'Now I'm going to have to clear that up. You complete cretin.'

Mike's apology is lost in the ferocious cloud of rage coming from Williams.

'You good for nothing loony. You psycho lunatic. You mental loony.'

Although he seems to be running out of descriptive words, it is plain to me that the one who appears mad is not my friend.

'Sorry.'

Mike's soft voice finds a temporary gap in Williams' ranting.

'Sorry?' He pauses either for effect or to emphasise his anger. 'Sorry? You lot don't deserve any of this, it's wasted on the likes of you. You're all fucking insane and mad.'

I find it hard to ignore his idiotic description as Williams makes his way to the bench, avoiding the puddle of varnish.

'I'll tell you what sorry gets you, shall I?' He doesn't wait for a response and picks up the magazine rack. 'See this?'

Williams raises the magazine rack and hurls it onto the floor. It hits where the floor meets the bench. Hours of careful attention, of personal pleasure, of diligent application; the topic of many proud conversations and of communal expectation, crushed in a second. Williams is not satisfied though, and he leaps on the damaged wood. He wants to ensure that

Mike's achievement is finished in a way that none of us had expected today. He stamps a black boot, demolishing the project, grinding it with his heel. He leaves scuff marks on a now unrecognisable work.

Before any of us are able to react, we watch Williams as his enraged eyes scan the room.

'And as for that fucking noise you make with that stupid guitar…'

This is not the first time Williams has said that to Mike, but this time I know it is different.

I watch as Williams marches across the department. He picks up Mike's guitar from where it is leaning against the radiator. He takes a while to examine it. I see a there is a grin forming on his thin lips. He starts to cackle and for a moment, I think he is about to make another joke. Something about Mike's inefficiency, or his tuneless efforts at guitar playing. Mike is also watching the events. He is wide-eyed, not wanting to take his gaze off Williams. Not wanting to take his gaze off his guitar, more like. He diverts his attention off the scene and glances over at me. I read the apprehension in his face.

Williams stops laughing and lets out a cough. He coughs on the guitar and then nods at it. Before we can say or do anything, he lofts it above his head.

Mike's favourite thing in all the world is suspended. It is like a sacrificial scene from the Bible.

In a swift arc, Williams brings the guitar down onto the hard floor with all his effort. I watch his eyes bulging, his veins once again standing out on his head.

Around his temples, his knees quake momentarily before he starts the downward movement. There is a crash, a splintering sound. Pieces of delicate wood rebound from the floor and as the strings are released from their perfectly tuned tension. A discordant twang of sadness rings through the department. The shattered wood and untethered steel lie on the floor like a car crash.

I can't take it anymore. I have watched him torture poor Sid for so long. It was bad enough when I watched his vicious face when Millie arrived at the Box Shop unannounced. And now he is doing this to Mike. Remember that time when I told you about the blood pumping around my head? Well it is happening again only this time it is rushing about my arms, my torso, my legs. The fury displaces the pain in my chest.

I look down at the bench and pick up the first thing that I see. Williams is leering at Mike, enjoying his moment. In a motion that catches Williams by surprise, I jab the screwdriver into his neck. It is like stabbing into a leg of pork. He makes a gasping noise as his eyes register the shock, his hand feels for the tool. Blood spills down onto his shirt collar, first as a trickle and then more steadily. The pattern forms a bloom on his shirt. Like broccoli. He instinctively pulls at the tool, but before he can withdraw it I pick up a chisel and drive it into his ribcage. He screams but it is low intensity. He is weak, I always knew it.

I don't have time to look at the others, my focus is on Williams. There is a lightness in my head that is strangely pleasurable. I look at the nails and the blades on the bench. Williams has fallen to his knees, his white shirt is now almost entirely red. The blood pools with the varnish. It looks like treacle. The two liquids don't mix. It is quite a contrast against the sawdust. He is gasping, wanting to say something, but he won't ever be hurling another insult. I mean to finish the bastard off for good.

My final weapon of choice is a convenient hammer. Having just had a demonstration of how to lift something and smash it down, I swing the hammer towards his head. It catches him slightly above and behind his ear. A hammer blow, you might say.

Crimson splatters all over my apron and up my arms. There is a hole, only a small one, but enough to show me the white of his skull. Blood spurts from all over Williams' body, it covers his face, hands and clothing. The hammer has pieces of skin and grey hairs on the metal. The force of the blow causes Williams to oscillate. Then he starts to topple in slow motion like an old tree.

When he finally hits the floor, his face crunches onto the concrete and rebounds. His groaning doesn't last long. His body twitches. I see the blood oozing from his mouth and I am impressed by the brightness. I stand over him, my chest is rising and falling, my heart dancing inside. There is a swooshing sound in my ears and I am lost in my own space.

When I look up, Mike is motionless. Although he has his hand over his mouth, I can see pleasure registering in his eyes. The room is silent, except for the gurgling death throes of the man who will not trouble us anymore. I am not sure that when the Beatles sang that song about happiness being a warm gun they meant it this way, but it works.

'Well,' says Sid. 'That's the end of him.'

Then he laughs, and it is a hearty laugh that will last forever...

### *One of my Poems*

*In the torrent of fear*
*through the void of eternity*
*In the torrent of fear*
*falls a special tear*

# Afterword

Writing a book on an evocative topic such as mental hospital life involves a lot of considerations, not least of which is the portrayal of the players in the system. The odd behaviour that Tim describes: the cotton wool head man, the mismatched clothing, the lack of concern for privacy, these are standard features of a mental hospital narrative. As a patient, Tim has licence to freely express his thoughts. Nevertheless, he remains connected as a person to his fellow patients.

There are many fictional works that amplify the characteristics and experiences of the cast to heighten the drama, but *Threeways* is an honest account of the trials of living in a long-term mental hospital, told in the Cromwellian spirit of 'warts and all'. That said, I have attempted through Tim to portray the characters in this book as sensitively as possible without losing the edge that realism provides. As a mental health professional, ethical considerations were always vying with literary forces in the depiction of the characters in the story. Ultimately, I wanted to retain as much dignity as possible in a setting of stark exposure and scrutiny that stripped people of their basic rights to privacy and humanity.

Although *Threeways* is about inner and outer worlds (as Tim makes clear), it goes beyond the power and control debate, and the 'us and them', because it is also a story of kindness flourishing in a place you might least expect it. Tim possesses a naive awareness, a phrase which sounds like an oxymoron. What I mean is that he has a consciousness of those around him, so his story has empathy. When it comes to the outside, however, he knows his skills would be challenged. That is one of the reasons he fails to engage with Ron's efforts.

Mental health issues span a range of social, political, economic and psychological concerns. The idea that a system can be used to control a section of society is, and always has been, a powerful one. This novel tackles serious issues which touch on personal liberty, control, and power, but I also wanted to show the strength of spirit, to show that enduring goodness could exist in a place of apparent hopelessness.

## The ending

I hesitated over the ending that some might misinterpret as 'mad person goes mad'. An uncritical reading might suggest that Tim has 'reverted to type', but my intention was far subtler than a blatant attempt to reinforce a social stereotype. What you chose to take from this work depends on your reading of it. Whether you see Tim's actions as part of his illness, or as a sacrifice for his friends, or a reaction to his own impending death, or even due to the anxiety concerning the plan to move him, it's up to you.

## HISTORICAL NOTE
### The Asylum System

As is often the case with efforts that have gone before, we now look back on the asylum system with a sense of collective shame. This is something we do when we consider that we have progressed. We also look back at the terrible water 'treatments', ECT and lobotomy with disgust, just as we may look back in years to come at the poisonous chemicals liberally dispensed to recipients who are left to live with the consequences.

In the novel, Tim imagines the conversation of future historians, who wonder how such a system could possibly have been conceived. We are already asking such questions.

Before the advent of asylum system in Britain, people suffering mental anguish were cared for in a haphazard arrangement of Poor Laws, local parishes and private madhouses. There were several early asylums, St Lukes in London, the York asylum and, of course, Bethlam Hospital, or Bedlam, that byword for madness. Bedlam has existed since 1247 and has moved at least twice in its time. It has been the subject of numerous plays, novels and artwork, Hogarth's *The Rake's Progress* being a notable example of the latter.

Towards the end of the century in Georgian Britain, a number of what were called 'private madhouses' were established. These were largely unregulated (although attempts at doing so were enshrined in the Madhouses Act of 1774) and inmates were often subject to profound ill-treatment.

This all changed in the 19<sup>th</sup> century with the asylum building programme. Whether you believe the asylum system was a humanitarian endeavour or the efforts to enforce conformity, or even something in between, depends on your viewpoint. Readers are directed towards Kathleen Jones for the former view and the work of sociologist Andrew Scull for the latter

Whatever the case, after a stuttering start, with the Asylums Act of 1808, which permitted for the raising of rates for voluntary building works, the system in the Britain began in earnest with the County Asylums Act of 1845 (passed simultaneously with the 1845 Lunacy Act). This act now *required* every county to build an establishment. These places were often out of town, hidden from view behind high walls, and they were massive. Just as Tim describes, in fact.

The crisis started almost as soon as they were finished being built. It was also evident early on that these grand places were becoming a dumping ground, a place in which inconvenient members of society (of all kinds) could be relegated. Thus corralled into the warehouses for the mad, the system started to struggle with the overwhelming numbers of inmates.

It didn't take long for the in-patient population to rise to serious levels. For example, London's famous Colney Hatch hospital, also known as Friern Barnet, opened with enormous capacity, with room for 1000 patients. A decade later, there was double that number.

Overcrowding was a familiar problem in every asylum without exception, and this made for expensive running costs and problems with staffing.

There were other reasons for this surge in population, including the reclassification of certain behaviours as mental illness. 'Habitual drunkenness', for example. (There was even a Habitual Drunkards Act passed in 1879) Such efforts suggested a pandemic of madness. Similar scaremongering still goes on, think about ADHD, OCD, anxiety disorders, they seem so commonplace that would be forgiven for thinking the whole world has gone mad. The 'medicalisation' thesis suggests that psychiatry is lowering the bar as to what they choose to label as illness. (See Richard Bentall and Rapley for discussions on this.)

The asylums moved from curative to custodial when the realisation that the original hopes of cure were optimistic, and this led to demoralisation and despondency in the asylums. Control was a tricky issue, and despite the imposition of strict rules and routines, staff had little time for therapeutic endeavour. Cases of abuse and maltreatment were becoming commonplace at the end of the 19$^{th}$ century, despite the Lunacy Commissioners inspecting conditions at the hospitals. In fact, the Lunacy Act of 1890 expressed pessimism with regard to treatment, suggesting that the mad should be kept well away from society.

The Mental Treatment Act of 1930, as its name suggests, had more of a focus on treatment for all patients. The apparently more enlightened attitude saw open-door policies implemented in many hospitals (the name change from asylum to mental hospital had occurred in the 1920s). In-patient populations peaked sometime around here, but failed to decline in significant numbers.

Just as there is controversy about the motives regarding the establishment of the asylum system, so it goes for the policy of closure (also referred to as decarceration and deinstitutionalisation). The 1959 Mental Health Act heralded the inevitable demise of a system over one hundred years old, but the reasons for this change are many. People often cite the so-called 'pharmacological revolution.' This refers to the advent of the drugs developed in the wake of the accidental discovery that the antihistamine chlorpromazine was able to subdue people with an agitated presentation. Huge numbers of similar compounds were developed, promoted by the twin powers of Big Pharma and medicine. The mythology about successful treatment was so pervasive that it is still widely accepted by the public (and many psychiatrists), as fact. Not only did these drugs allow pharmaceutical companies to make money, but because physical treatment fits with medical model of disease/illness, it legitimises the position of medical specialists, presenting a veneer of science. With this and the advent of legal powers in the 1959 act, psychiatrists solidified medical dominance over mental health.

This pharmacological argument though, is too convenient, because there were also significant financial incentives to a closure movement, that is without question. Pretty much every mental hospital was expensive and many were in need of serious reparation.

In truth, the attitude towards mental health problems had been shifting for some time, with a greater emphasis on integration and interest in developing methods of coping if not curing. These were certainly reinforced by the new medications (which, it should be acknowledged, help many sufferers live a life they might not otherwise, it's just that psychiatry is not always honest about what the drugs actually do, which is to alter presentation) and the move towards in-patient units and community facilities. The rise in awareness about social factors also helped refocus attention.

The 1960s and 70s saw the advent of anti-psychiatry, in the works of David Cooper and R D Laing (although they both denied the term), which helped to move the critique onto the system rather than the patient. This movement was a powerful indictment of the traditional system, and helped in no small way to undermine the status quo.

Perhaps one of the most significant factors in recognising the harm that these institutions were doing was the work of American sociologist Erving Goffman and his ilk. Goffman's work *Asylums*, dealt with the negative effects of what he termed 'total institutions', including mental hospitals. Along with Russell Barton's work *Institutional Neurosis*, and in Britain, and J K

Wing's papers on what he called 'institutionalism', the public were shown the terrible effect of long-term institutional living. Patients were revealed as shuffling, hopeless characters, devoid of volition and stripped of dignity and who acquire a significantly different moral code to the rest of us. Tim shows us lots of examples of such patients, including his 'man in the corridor'. The patients' labelling of their own social club as *Fags and Shags* is something of an ironic commentary on the phenomenon. In many cases, the passivity with which patients came to accept the routines and rules were as much to blame for the apathy demonstrated within the hospitals as the symptoms of any illness. In fact, Tim and his friends at Threeways belong to a group described by Foucault in *Madness and Civilization* as being in a 'minority status'.

There were associated factors, such as the hospital scandals of the 1960s, 70s and 80s, outlined in J P Martin's book, *Hospitals in Trouble,* which when added to the former problems meant that the old system had run its course. Some relics of the old system can still be seen, readers can find a great pictorial depiction in Mark Davis' 2014 book, *Asylum.*

The replacement system of 'community care' was, frankly, a complete let down. As it was pointed out, 'simply changing the locus of bad care will not create good care.' (Borus, J.F. Deinstitutionalization of the chronically mentally ill. *N. Eng. J. Med.,* 1981, *305*, 339-342.)

While it would be hoped that 21<sup>st</sup> century mental health services are more flexible, sadly, we still hear too many stories about inadequate funding, pressures on hard-pressed staff, and service-users who must deal with the consequences.

## A Word on 'Treatment' in Psychiatry

The continued quest for causation has led successive theorising about what 'treatments' might be effective. Put simply, the problem is that when you do not know what the cause of distress is, it is hard to know how to treat the matter. Through the ages, the mad have been assailed with various strange and dangerous speculative physical procedures in the hope of cure.

For example:
In the 17th century, the mad were subjected to bloodletting, emetics and purging, based on theories of illness descended from humors.

In the 18th and 19th centuries, patients were chained and manacled, they were beaten and whipped and whirled about in an attempt to 'shock' them back to sanity. They were also subject to cold showers and given experimental potions in acts of medical quackery.

The late 19th century saw conflicting theories of the mind, with psychoanalysis developing at one end, and biological theories of putative pathology on the other.

By the 1920s, patients were having parts of their bodies (teeth, spleen, tonsils, colons) removed in the belief that they might be the cause of illness. (The 'focal sepsis' theory is detailed in *Madhouse*, by Andrew Scull. See also e.g. Davies, below.)

In the 1930s onwards, patients underwent insulin 'therapy', where they were placed in a coma in an attempt to quieten their madness.

In the 1950s, ECT (electroconvulsive therapy, or electric shock treatment) was given to patients on no other basis than 'it seemed to work'. (See: C Newnes (Ed): *This is Madness*, 1999.)

As if these practices were don't sound strange enough in today's world, some hospitals even tried malaria as a cure. Imagine that. They allowed mosquitoes to bite patients and infect them, hoping their illness would go away.

And let's not forget lobotomy, where a Portuguese man (Egas Moniz) suggested that cutting parts of the brain would help (with an ice-pick and a mallet, in the case of practitioner Walter Freeman), and the craze caught on. Now if that's not madness, I don't know what is. (Moniz received a Nobel Prize in 1949, but as Scull tells us in *Madness: A Very Short Introduction*, due to the backlash, Moniz lived out his life 'reviled as a moral monster'.)

Tim makes repeated reference to the reliance on medication and the harmful effects on him and his friends. Sadly, even today, in the 21st century, millions of pills are given out purporting to act in specific ways on specific diseases.

As a claim, this has three problems:

**1** The medicine is not targeted

**2** The evidence will point to the fact that the diseases they refer to are not separate and distinct entities

**3** In most cases, there is little evidence of specific physical illness to back up the claim of a disease process

Additionally, the evidence, such that it is, suggests little or no benefit over harmless placebo in terms of efficacy.

(The incidence of 'publication bias' can be read about in Richard Bentall's book cited below.)

The situation is summed up by Tim, who talks of patients as 'chlorpromazine slot machines, where the medication is fed in with no idea of the result but in hope of a jackpot'.

Finally, consider this…

*Despite the advances in the biomedical and psychological sciences that have occurred since then, many of the assumptions made*

*about mental illness made by Victorian psychiatrist continue to guide the practice of mental health professionals today'* (R. Bentall, Doctoring the Mind, 2009)

*'In spite of claims of dramatic advances in the understanding and treatment of mental illness, patients are doing no better now than they did a hundred years ago.'* (L Johnstone, Users and Abusers of Psychiatry, 1995.)

These two quotes provide a shocking wake-up call for those who assume psychiatry has all the answers. Unfortunately, the cyclical nature of psychiatry means that the issues of stigma, of the withdrawal of liberty, and of self-determination, are as acute now as they were in the 1970s. (One might argue the 1870s.) The fact that the victims of these systemic consequences are no longer confined to a mental hospital should not disguise the fact that damage can still be inflicted. The repeated failures of any system, whether that is 'community care' or medical 'treatment' are brought into focus on those at the sharp end. In other words, the sufferer and their family.

### Reading suggestions:
**Asylum system**: Andrew Scull is excellent (*Madhouses, mad-doctors, and madmen: The social history of psychiatry in the Victorian era. Also Social order / mental disorder. Also, The most solitary of afflictions: Madness and society in Britain, 1700-1900.*

An older volume of books: Bynum, W.F., Porter, R. and Shepherd, M. *The Anatomy of Madness: Volumes 1, 2 and 3.*

**Institutionalisation**: Erving Goffman's *Asylums* is a classic study of institutions.

Russell Barton, *Institutional Neurosis.*

J.K. Wing, 'Institutionalism in mental hospitals', British Journal of Social and Clinical Psychology, 1(1), pp. 38-51.

**Bedlam**: Katherine Arnold's book *Bedlam: London and its Mad.*

Mike Jay's *This Way Lies Madness.*

**Closure and community care**: Phil Brown, *The transfer of care: Psychiatric deinstitutionalization and its aftermath.*

Kathleen Jones, *Experience in Mental Health.*

Borus, J.F. Deinstitutionalization of the chronically mentally ill. *N. Eng. J. Med.*, 1981, 305, 339442.

**Treatment**: *The Myth of the Chemical Cure*, by psychiatrist Joanna Moncrieff is iconoclastic.

David Healy's *Let Them Eat Prozac* is typically insightful.

Focal sepsis: Andrew Scull, *Madhouse: A tragic tale of megalomania and modern medicine.*

**Medicalisation**: Rapley, M., Moncrieff, J. and Dillon, J. (eds.) *De-medicalizing misery: Psychiatry, psychology and the human condition.*

**General critical texts**: Michel Foucault, *Madness and Civilisation.*

Thomas Szasz, *The manufacture of madness.* Also *The myth of mental illness: Foundations of a theory of personal conduct.*

James Davies', *Cracked,* and Richard Bentall's *Doctoring the Mind* are excellent critiques of psychiatry and its failings.